Date With Death

By Daniel Fisher

When Death comes for you, you better be prepared!

I

As road trips went, this one started much rougher than the guys would have liked. Already they were delayed some six hours from their targeted departure time due in large part to an inordinate amount of primping and preening on three of the companion's part. After that, the actual ride should have been a no brainer, unfortunately, the driver fit that description to a tee, and the downward spiral began in earnest.

Dustin didn't really mind seeing as he wasn't in a big rush to get to Santa Fe. So he sat quietly in the middle of the backseat with his earbuds reading a book while pretending not to listen to the pointless bickering.

From the start, there was near-constant bitching and moaning about a million little things between Gary, the driver pushing forty who was behaving like a four year old and Amir, who was roughly the same age but better able to hold it together in the passenger seat. It would have been funny if they weren't so pedantic.

Dustin felt they were acting like petty alpha males trying to establish dominance over this pack of captive buffoons. They might as well spray to mark their territory. Who knew, Amir's boyfriend Jordon cruising on his phone in the backseat may like the golden showers.

The latest round after an already tedious amount of driving was that Gary got caught up going round and round the rickety old bridge that connects Wheeling by a tenuous degraded string to the rest of the world. A bridge, that if he followed directions Dustin gave to Gary's lover Arman, they could have avoided completely. Much the same way as people who reside in Wheeling do whenever possible.

But that would be too easy. Instead, Gary became flustered by Amir's incessant nagging to "get in the next lane" in his ear. Gary would, in the wrong direction, to which Jordon, who could have been cast as the sexy, jock bully, background character in any number of angsty teen dramas, hurled insults masquerading as critiques from behind. More barking in the ear to go the other way, and so on. The people most in danger seemed to be the other cars being thrust out of the vehicle's path. Nerves frayed, stuck in rush hour traffic, along with the driver's last-second course corrections made the situation a nail biter on the two-lane death trap of rusting metal. Judging by how it creaked and teetered it may well have collapsed any second, sending them and many of the other frustrated souls to their deaths at the bottom of this desolate ravine.

Dustin wasn't worried, mostly because with all the insults and criticisms thrown his way, Gary was oblivious to any of it. He was driving on pure ego, simply to impress Arman, looking cross, scrunched in the backseat next to Dustin. Possibly constipated, Dustin wasn't entirely certain but he appeared troubled either way.

"I got this!" Gary exclaimed, careening into the far right lane, causing a smaller two-door to veer into the railing. Gary didn't see them so in his mind they didn't exist. Arman, becoming intensely frustrated, smacked his forehead into the passenger side window for several minutes.

Well, it wasn't his stomach. Dustin thought to himself.

By the grace of some unearthly power or stupid sheer luck, Gary managed to squeeze and clip the cars and trucks cramming the roadway, making it back onto Seventy-West and out of the pseudo-apocalyptic themepark known as West Virginia.

Strangely, he somehow managed to have a misplaced sense of accomplishment, smiling smugly to Arman. Dustin instantly pictured Gary begging for a treat and a belly-rub. He made a low chuckle, gaining the attention of Arman. He apparently had a similar notion.

"Told ya, I'd get us through." Smiling through his porn star good looks, shining veneers and slight graying on the sides which enhanced Gary's soft blue eyes. Gary sparkled for his man. Arman made a face like he wanted to hit Gary with a shoe.

"We wouldn't have even had to go this way if you'd just followed the directions!" Arman screeched, his high was gone completely, replaced only with a high pitched squeal. Gary waved him off. His thoughts moved on, probably to how Arman would make it up to him later.

Before they left Scranton, Arman smoked a joint to maintain calm on the ride. An hour later when Gary, Amir, and Jordon were squabbling about the placement of the bags in the back of the battered black SUV, Arman lit up another to keep calm. After that, the guys worked up a thirst unconcerned about Arman and forgetting Dustin was there completely. So cocktails for an hour, then each one had to 'freshen up' so another hour of primping and flushing and preening, so when it came time to actually leave Arman was way too high to drive.

He'd have preferred Dustin drive because he knew Dustin forever, and Dustin was pretty much the only responsible person in the group. At least the only one with any kind of steady job, or steady anything considering Dustin had to hold Arman upright at that point.

On a good day, Gary barely acknowledged Dustin, and this wasn't a good day for Gary. Dustin didn't mind it though, he thought of Gary much like an old tire iron. A tool you may never need, but handy in a pinch. However, you're better off not having to rely on it, so it just sits there.

"So much for a romantic getaway," Arman whispered in Dustin's ear. Unlike Jordon on the left passenger side, Arman was trying to give Dustin a little room to move.

"I'm sorry what?" He pulled the earbud out and smirked.

"I said..."

"Oh, I heard what you said, I just believed you were smart enough to realize, nothing about this trip is going to be romantic, especially with Gary involved." Dustin's smirk grew with a gleeful menace. Arman snorted.

"What's happening?" Gary moaned from the driver's seat. Wanting to be the center of Arman's world, not of conversation with someone else.

"Never you mind. Shut up! Because... that's what." Arman made a snotty pinched nose snarl to Gary. Turning back to Dustin. "I'm almost ready to take your headphones and strangle him." Whispering in delight.

"No, don't do that. The cord would probably tear before he stops breathing." Dustin sounding so deadpan while rubbing the wire tubing with his fingers, Arman looked like he wasn't sure if his friend was joking or not. "Besides we'll be stopping soon, just release him into the wild."

"Funny, what a wasted day. This sucks."

"It'll be fine. We'll pull over soon and can start fresh in the morning."

"Where is there to pull over?" Arman gazed out the window at a whole lot of hills.

"We're about to hit Ohio, the entire highway is like a strip-mall until Indiana. Unless he gets lost on some back road, then we're doomed." Side eyeing the driver.

"Don't even joke about that, he'll probably run us into a ditch or something. I won't do so well being stuck in Rural Ohio."

"No one does well in rural Ohio, besides its getting dark so all those shiny lights along the road will flicker and gleam to hold Gary's attention." Dustin curled his lip.

"What?" Gary bellowed, swerving some.

"Pay attention to the road asshole!" Amir, jostled, just as he was settling into rest, would now make it his mission to get on Gary's last nerve.

And he did, Dustin put the earpiece back in, turned up the volume and began singing to himself. The next few hours would be filled with some quality bitch time between Gary and Amir. But eventually, they'd tucker themselves out and pull off the highway for the night. Dustin chuckled at the thought of them.

He'd known Arman from childhood and had a really solid friendship. Arman was super amped when Dustin informed him that his parents invited the group out to Santa Fe. Dustin could easily have flown out to see the family, but he proposed a road trip instead.

Talking Arman into volunteering his hand me down SUV, an intrepid vehicle that was a gift from his father was a piece of cake. Arman jumped at the chance to do a cross country in the old death trap. The ancient auto was originally meant for his sister. However due to all the late nite joyrides when they were young, the SUV suffered a lifetime of cosmetic damage in only a few short years. From scratches and dents, front end and bumper damage, to some rather inexplicable set of flashing police lights added around homecoming their junior year of high school, Arman's father gave up and made him take the truck.

Growing up together Arman became a staple around Dustin's house, he knew the family pretty well, and Dustin's parents very well, considering he spent much of his free time in high school smoking weed with them. To the present day, Arman could not understand how they weren't locked up or dead from all the trouble they got into. Dustin knew but wasn't talking. Best not to soil Arman's view of the world until he had to.

Dustin met Amir through Arman in college. Amir began dating Jordon shortly after that if you could call it dating. More like hiring the trick, falling for the trick and asking the trick to move in. Somewhere along the way, they became an item, so Jordon was inescapable. He was an acquired taste for Dustin, selfish, brooding and kind of a trash whore.

Gary wasn't much better, he and Arman met in a dark bathroom during a Harrisburg pride bar crawl a few years back. Then they ran into each other again in a gym locker room back in Scranton. Dustin was thankful he had a strong constitution, otherwise thinking about Gary being naked Gary, would have made him hurl. He stopped going to Gary's gym after seeing them in the steamroom, some horrors were just too much to bear.

With the sun set and the night in full swing, the dirt-covered black box on wheels careened its way from strip mall to strip mall halfway through Ohio. Everyone was tired from the ride, wanting out of the vehicle and wanting very much away from each other for a stretch. Except for Dustin, he was used to this discomfort. These were theoretically his friends. Unfortunately, they were people who only noticed him when it was convenient for them to do so. And Arman, Dustin gave him wide latitude for associating with the other guys. Deep down, like really deep down in Gary's case, he knew they were good people at heart.

Dustin, Arman, and Amir came together early on in college with a mutual desire to create an interfaith coalition of gay men for social justice. The mission got derailed quickly as Amir, who only used his faith to pick up liberal dudes, would entice Arman to go out bar hopping instead of making any real change in the world. And because it was easy to convince Dustin to be his wingman, the only thing they managed to change was their morning routine to adjust to the hangovers.

Amir met Jordon on one of those outings, got his business card, and after many calls hiring him for late-night massages, they were a couple. For Dustin to call Jordon an "escort" would be generous. But he did have ambition, Jordon wanted to have the 'fab life' and would do anything (or anyone) to get it. So while the rest simmered, Jordon was plotting his next salacious move.

Unexpectedly bellowing in Gary's ear "when are we stopping" scanning his phone and back. "Where's Edina?" He added, the profile on his screen consuming his interest.

Dustin, acting as though he honestly believed Jordon was asking him, raised his arm to remove his earpiece, knocking Jordon's hand, causing him to swipe left instead of right.

"Dude! What the hell?" Anger spitting from Jordon pouty lips. "Now I have to start all over." Jordon fumed while Dustin played it off like it was a complete accident. Including the obligatory shrug. "Whatever, I'll try again tomorrow." Jordon got flustered and closed the app.

Poor Jordon, Dustin thought. A classic American beauty, not the brightest guy, but earnest in his shallowness. Bald as a baby's butt and a man with enough compromising pictures to make even the most lecherous of priest's limp from the sheer amount of gratuitous smut.

Dustin wasn't in the mood to wait around while they'd have to file a missing person's report on the guy. Sure he wasn't in a rush to get to Santa Fe, but that didn't mean he wanted to be stuck with Amir, sobbing and heartbroken at losing his lover in the middle of an Ohio suburb.

"Look there's a place up ahead, three miles," Amir called out the sign on the highway for an exit with a few choice hotel brands, plenty of gas and food options. It was the most logical option.

"Naw, I like that one." Gary gunned it, pulling off at the one-mile exit for the less well traveled sign. Up a steep ramp just overlooking the highway on either side, like the road cut this tiny burg in half, Gary pulled recklessly into the 'White Swallow' Inn's mostly empty parking lot. A dumpy and run down looking establishment that may, or may not have been, the backdrop for several horror movies, and almost certainly the set of many seventies porno's.

"You're an idiot." Amir snorted.

"It's classic."

"It's disgusting." Arman chirped, eyeballing Gary with animosity.

"There's no wi-fi." Jordon, now upset for a new reason, flailed his phone about.

"And it's settled, I'll get us a room." Gary bolted from the car, taking the keys with him. At least part of him knew they'd leave his ass behind. Arman was about to ask Dustin to hotwire the SUV, but, then he pondered what might happen if they got pulled over? If they'd had to wait too long Dustin would have informed him not to worry about such petty details.

Sadly for Arman, any hope of abandoning Gary was dashed when he returned giggling the room key in hand. He snatched his lover by the arm as he cautiously exited the car, dragging Arman to the nearest entryway into this heinous, cheap-ass, no-tell, motel nightmare in the middle of Ohio. Dustin shrugged and followed. How bad was this going to be he wondered.

Able finally to take a little time away from his work a day life, and with the hopes of attracting the other *like that'll ever happen* he mused, Dustin decided to dust off some of his special and not often discussed skills. With a blink, he broadened the visual spectrum to reveal how the room really looked. Beneath the surface, so to speak.

These talents allowed him to view worlds unseen by his fellow companions much like a human blacklight. Slowly at first, pale neon blue auras sparked into life, then in short order, the wisps of black, popping and evaporating, and finally everything in between. The psychic ash converging into focus around them.

No one was that thrilled about being the first one inside, so Dustin stepped up gazing at the outside and visibly in any spectrum, stained and nasty entryway. The exterior was covered with bubbling layers of paint, only partially camouflaging aged stains of biological matter, none of which Dustin cared to speculate on.

Arman hesitated to go anywhere near it, but because of Gary's larger frame managed to wrangler the smaller human shield toward the door. Jordon and Amir held back, they were at least smart enough to let their friends die first if anything was to spring out at the group.

Upon opening the door and flipping on the switch Dustin's eyes became drawn immediately to the interior, which was much more disgusting than the doorway, as hard as that was to believe.

Inside, he could see how the room was merely wiped down, not in any way truly disinfected. DNA and fibrous material strewn haphazardly over every surface, their prints telling story after story of depraved and gruesome acts that happened over the decades.

Blues and black spots, like images from a bad acid trip flowered along the walls and ceiling. A cluster of decayed memories paced the room, unaware of ever being alive, not knowing they were dead. Years of faded outlines, those lingering afterthoughts, or as anyone who only catches a glimpse calls them, ghosts; were abundant. Like blurs under multiple layers of dust covered glass, they were just the residue of those who perished here and near to this location. The residual shell from the human garbage they once were.

Dustin had experience with all this and worse, so he wasn't shaken by any of the popping and oozing otherness. He was a tad disgusted by what was moving over the twin beds in the room, very clear evidence of something alive.

"There's bedbugs." He said, pointing at the nearest bed.

Good timing too, Gary was about to fly sideways onto the far bed disrupting their quiet community and contaminating his clothes.

"You sure." Arman leaned in, he believed Dustin, he simply wanted to make sure he heard correctly as he backed away slowly, making for the exit.

"Oh yeah." Dustin allowed his eyes to return to the standard visual spectrum; frankly, he thought the room had more character with the trippy colors. Moving to the pillow of the nearest bed he pointed out some small moving spots.

"I'm not staying here!" An irate Jordon spittled in Amir's face, angered by the thought of this vile place.

"At least we can shower." Dustin said softly, knowing full well they would hear him.

"How? Those things could be everywhere." Gary bemoaned to Arman, looking past Dustin entirely like he wasn't even present.

After rolling his eyes, making a sympathetic brow movement to Dustin for being ignored, and taking a deep breath, he responded to the childish man. "The bathroom's tiled. And we have our own towels."

"Dibs." Jordon paused his storming out just long enough to call it, then raced to get his shower bag. Amir followed after, shaking his head at Gary who simply stood there, staring at the bathroom for a few minutes longer than one would have thought was needed to put two and two together.

Jordon and Amir showered first, together. Dustin would have thought they would have taken longer to finish, but he was glad they got done with whatever they were doing in quick fashion. Then Gary had his turn. He wanted Arman to join him, but Arman wasn't fond of Gary at the moment so he took a polite pass. Washing away his anger, Arman went next and finally, Dustin got a chance to wash the day away. He was just pleased there was still hot water, otherwise, he may have had to get upset.

Exiting the room and its bloodthirsty occupants, Dustin paced to the SUV. Amir and Jordon had snuggled up in their respective seats, and Gary and Arman were saying goodnight with a much too public display of affection. Tons of making out and ample grouping, about all Dustin could do to keep his stomach from flipping was turn away and watch the sky. Clearly, Arman had a soft spot for Gary, and it seemed Gary just had a soft head. All the troubles of the day, was like water under the bridge. It was sweet and everything, but Dustin didn't want to see any part of it.

Eventually, the two separated before they'd have to shower off the spunk, and settled into the vehicle. Dustin, not wanting to be trapped between Arman and Jordon and Jordon's feet, curled up on the windshield with his towel tucked behind his head. He was certain no one and nothing would disturb his peace while he slept.

As the first to rise, Dustin understood the group would want to set out as soon as possible. So he had hours to kill. He set out at a leisurely pace across the busy highway to a small diner on the other side, and after enjoying some terrific waffles and grabbing a to-go order for Arman, who he knew would need food, he moseyed to a convenient store a ways down to get some provisions for the road. Dustin returned as his companions were piling out of the SUV, grumpy and achy. Jordon could be heard bitching as he exited the vehicle. "It starts early." Dustin murmured to himself.

"I'm just saying its common knowledge to check hotel rooms for bedbugs."

Dustin wasn't sure if anyone other than Jordon, who had spent many a night in cheap hotels, would have thought it to be common knowledge, so he kept tight-lipped about it and passed off a coffee to Arman.

"Thank you." Looking around to find where Dustin procured it. Spotting the diner in the distance past all the traffic, Arman looked suspiciously at Dustin and back to his coffee. As per usual Dustin's expression was one of mild contentment, however before Arman could ask any questions he honestly didn't want answers to, Dustin passed him a paper bag.

"This will most likely be the only buttered biscuits you get on this trip, so enjoy." Smirking.

"Rude!" Arman scrunched up his face.

"What about us?" Gary barked, thus evaporating any kind feelings Arman carried over from the night before.

Dustin handed Amir a plastic bag and the three other guys went to town on protein bars and energy drinks while Dustin sat with Arman in the backseat enjoying his coffee.

"He almost made me forget he was being a douche." Arman lamented.

"That's his charm, not many men know how to swallow their own foot whole." Dustin caused Arman to chortle into his coffee.

II

Toward the end of a second rough travel day, the guys were stewing in testosterone and butt sweat. Although the air conditioning was doing a wonderful job, the close quarters and slow stop and start traffic around Indianapolis was wearing everyone down. Add in some brooding and it was quickly becoming a toxic man stew.

Dustin was starting to feel like the only bun soaking up the juices at this sausage fest, so he tried to stay calm, singing a catchy electro-pop Chumbawamba song softly to himself, even as he was stuck once more between Arman, pensive over some such thing, probably Gary; and Jordon doing some intense man-spreading. For some reason Dustin didn't want to ponder about, the tensed up meat-slab to his left was doing some major clenching. The seat moving each time his ass contracted.

As the day continued speeding by faster than the traffic, Gary got fussier with each jolted stop from the bumper to bumper traffic. He'd managed to find his way into an endless maze of road construction, so he'd get angry and keep taking random exits, only to wind them back around on the bypass that should have been the shortcut through Indianapolis. What was causing such exasperation, was each time Gary would get back on the bypass, it would somehow be a few miles further back than where he'd exited.

Dustin wanted to give Gary a pass for trying, and blame the department of roads for this suburban circle of purgatory, however, sadly he had to admit Gary making the late summer Friday afternoon traffic worse, simply because he wouldn't take advice from his navigator Amir.

"There. Get over into the right lane." He'd say.

"No, if I go this way it'll cut back to seventy." Gary would snort.

"You already went that way and we ended up three miles back. On this same stretch!" And that would open the gates of bickering for another hour.

Dustin minded the nonstop bickering more than the delay, so when the tedious moaning started to be too much, he silently took a deep breath, exhaled with lips pursed, and like a cooling wind aimed it at the back of Gary's neck. The calm chill from the simple motion of air quieted Gary long enough to accept a suggestion that helped them out of the flyover states concrete version of the nine circles. Seemingly much later, the giant fiery ball in the sky hit dead on the windshield as they were leaving the Hoosier state and heading for the heart of the lonely country.

Setting quickly, the roads became more and more desolate, just one pair of taillights now in front. About the only thing to watch was Gary and Amir continue to squabble. Passing into Illinois they should have dropped that other conversation like a murder weapon down a storm drain. But no, they continued, adding to the discomfort. Dustin felt he could have perhaps added a touch more spice to the mixture of his cool breeze to calm the bitching and moaning. However, he was still a novice with certain things and didn't want to nudge too harshly. Too much and Gary could have taken on the personality of a crash test dummy, and that wouldn't work out so well for Dustin.

To him, Amir and Gary had many of the same attributes of an Arab, Israeli conflict. Each time they barked back and forth new and more hateful insults were thrown. Next it could be missiles and rocks. Except that Gary looked like a gym rat in a pride parade and could be the poster child for the Aryan nation, who in no way was able to use any kind of rocket launcher. He'd blow himself up on the first try. He was Jewish, but as the story went, he skipped out on his Bar mitzvah to go water skiing with his friends.

Then there was Amir, second generation Iranian, with no cultural ties to his country or history. Muslim, but then there was the whole using his faith to get his mosque worshipped thing. That was as much interest in his heritage as he had. Maybe the erotic poetry, but in English and on audio tape, read by a pornstar.

These guys were perfect for each other, at least to argue with, other than that, they weren't much use at all as far as Dustin was concerned. Outsiders to this supposed group of friends would say that Gary, Amir, Jordon, and Arman were massively attractive. Especially Arman.

Egyptian mom, Indian dad, born first generation American. He had stunning eyes, great features with a nice build. Sadly, to Dustin anyway, many a guy, the one driving in particular, treated Arman as if he was just a piece of meat, with no brain or thoughts to go along with the grey matter. So Arman stuck close to Dustin because he could actually have a conversation that wasn't about what someone wanted to do to him.

Folks engaging the guys as a group or individually, generally never noticed Dustin or what he looked like, if any combination of them were present. He just sort of blended into the background when his companions were in the room of a party or at a bar. He'd get hit on when he was alone, and had a good sense of self esteem, but when the guys would stroll in Dustin may as well been a potted plant in the corner. Again he didn't mind, he liked guys that were known to be unusual.

"Dustin... D-u-s-t-i-n..." Arman sang in his friend's ear. Dustin was lost in thought, a growing sneer developing on his mug.

Pulling out the earpiece, Dustin somehow managed to do a repeat of the night before and cause Jordon to lose his place trolling for paying dick.

"What the hell?" Irate, Jordon jerked up immediately. Dustin merely shrugged turning his attention to Arman as Jordon fumed.

"There you are. You were like a million miles away. Everything okay?" Arman inquired cautiously. It wasn't often Dustin looked upset, he was normally content or deadpan, the two expressions he showed the world.

"What? Yeah, I'm just reexamining some questionable life choices. And I blame you." Switching to a sarcastic smirk.

"What'd I do?" Genuinely stunned, Arman's deep brown eyes lit up in questions.

"Well..." Making side-eye at the boys in the front.

"Yeah, that was me. But I can explain..."

"You thought Amir was hot, so you talked to him, and this downward spiral continues all these years later. So here we are." Dustin smiled broadly.

"That's on you."

"How so?"

"You didn't stop me. You were and are, always so prim and proper. It's all your fault really... You're always so introverted, so I have to be the one who puts myself out there." Arman rebutted.

"Because I know what'll happen. Amir opened his mouth and his sexiness bled out like a gunshot victim." Dustin stuck his tongue out for added effect.

"Ew... You thought he was hot too. Come on."

"Uh, yeah but here we are six years later and still with the beard. Does he not have a chin? Plus, I mean, Jonnie apple core over there." Referring to Jordon on his other side. Who, when Arman glanced over at, looked like a slice of the American dream-sicle, seething with hatred for Dustin who disrupted his business. Again.

Ignoring Jordon's hatred completely Arman remarked. "I think we both know Amir doesn't have a chin."

"Hey!" Gary shouted from the front, turning his attention to Arman. "We're going to need gas soon."

"So!" Gary a tad too needy for Arman to bear was about to start in on his mate when Dustin smacked him on the shoulder.

Dustin's attention was drawn to a face behind Arman's reflection, outside the window. It wasn't so much a warning as a surprise hello from the inky blackness Dustin hoped to reconnect with.

"He needs to watch the road." Dustin spoke in a deep growling tone.

"Asshole! Watch the road!" Arman belched out, and just in time.

The taillights in front of them flashed an angry red as the driver veered off, stopping abruptly on the gravel emergency lane. Had it not been for Arman's shouting, Gary would have smacked directly into the back of the old blue pickup truck. Instead, he careened around and in front, as an object flew by the window. Hitting the brakes, they jostled inside the SUV and came to a halt between lanes on the barren highway. Had it been earlier, the roadway would have been busy and they would have paperwork to fill out due to a roadside fatality or four.

Nerves already rattled, it took several minutes for the group to settle down and process what just happened. Dustin not shaken by the events had already wriggled out of the vehicle without notice and was piecing together what transpired. Arman wondering why his door was open, popped out to see if the people in the pickup truck were alright. He received a less than warm reception when he addressed an older pasty couple in tragic outerwear. It didn't matter that he was wearing a snappy jean, tee shirt combo, Arman's black hair, and rich caramel skin stopped the pale folks in their tracks.

"Are you okay?" He asked. They responded with silence.

Jumping out of the passenger side, the old man and woman were stiffened even more by the likes of Amir. Standing no more than three feet away from the wreckage and the pickup truck, Dustin who was evidently invisible to everyone shook his head in annoyance, feelt it was safe to assume these people didn't have much experience with darker skinned folks.

They merely held each other tight looking at Arman and Amir in the sexy, but deadly terrorist role. Somehow armed with concealed explosives under their skin-tight clothes. Dustin decided he would go and explore what they hit and should let this lowest common denominator of Americana play itself out but he couldn't resist watching for a little while longer. He was now the one caught in the headlights.

"Floyd..." The woman whispered, but not very softly. Her twang was audible to Arman and Amir.

"Janice, calm down. Don't make any sudden movements..." Likewise, his belittling tone would have also been heard, Arman and Amir were no further away than Dustin.

The old man softened his grip on the female when Jordon rose out of the backseat, looking like a background actor in a truck commercial. He was even wearing a trendy blue and white American flag shirt. One of those chain store finds that male prostitutes generally wore to make them appear classier than they truly were. All that butch in the streets, sort of thing. But as Dustin knew from seeing way too much of his profile, Jordon was all pussycat in the sheets.

"Oh, thank god." The man praised a bit too loudly.

"But why is he traveling with them?" The woman asked. By the expressions Amir and Arman made, they'd her heard her.

"I don't know Janice, just stay calm."

III

Not wanting to ponder the stupid going on around him, Dustin weaved directly around the two locals and a bewildered Jordon unnoticed. If he was a serial killer, he thought to himself, he could easily stab any one of them and they wouldn't know where their attacker came from. Chuckling, Dustin was about to inquire what they hit. That surely would spoil the growing semi of pride, the man with an off the rack denim jeans-suit combo, was sporting for Jordon. However, when an exasperated Gary climbed out of the driver's seat with his 'smoldering' good looks, the older man about popped a full-on woody. Gravitating to the two white men like a politician to cash while his denim pants gravitated up his ass crack. He was deadset on getting *them* to investigate the damage to his bloodied front end.

Amir and Arman were attempting to offer helpful suggestions only to be eyeballed suspiciously by the elder woman seemingly set in her ways, clutching her sweater. Dustin felt it might be time to let this dead horse rest in peace and continue on the find what these folks hit. Dustin moseyed to the back of the pickup to investigate what was most likely dead or dying.

He'd seen the blur and something else, just a flash in the window. One that suggested an object died on impact. On the edge of the road about twenty feet back was a doe, lying on her side in the gravel. The last bits of life fading in the blinking hazard lights from the truck.

Not remotely interested in hearing about fenders and miscellaneous car parts, Arman searched about for Dustin. Not seeing him with the group or in the vehicle he paced down the road where Dustin was kneeling by the side of a limp looking mass. Moving in for a closer look he could see in the red flashing glow of the hazard lights Dustin had squatted down over an animal and heard him speaking softly. "Go with grace."

He made a small hand gesture on the doe's forehead, and then raised his head. And as he did, Dustin noticed something, not a blur this time, something much clearer. The doe was standing, next to a shadow, its bandaged black gauzy hand, petting the animals back. Slowly Dustin stood, smiling. To Arman, he looked a bit possessed. Still, almost robotic in how smooth and silent his moves were.

"It's good to see you." He said softly, almost a whisper. Arman heard but couldn't have.

"See who?" Attempting cautiously to get Dustin's attention. Arman didn't want to touch him, because he could have lost his mind, but perhaps he should have shaken him to snap him out of what outwardly looked like a trance.

"Nothing." Smiling broadly as the figure and the deer turned and moved out of phase.

Before departing into nothingness through a smokey fog, this shadow, tied and bound up like a mummy in black and blue-grey wrappings, wearing a shroud of smoke; turned and made what could best be described as a smile at Dustin. A smile, if someone went by the movement under the bandages on what might be considered a face. The impression of a smile at least.

"You alright?" Arman gently put his hand on Dustin's shoulder.

Turning to his friend, Dustin's face was calm and serene. "Yeah, I'm fine. The meat's no good. The doe ruptured its belly." He was looking just past Arman to the older gentleman walking toward them with a knife.

Not a stabbing knife, a hunting knife. Used to cut open and gut things. Hearing about the gut he cringed. "You sure about that?" With a look that read these city boys didn't know nothing about nothing.

"I am, it's spilled out. The intestines are leaking." Moving so the older man could get a better view. "You might be able to salvage the meat above the heart. And the pelts in fair shape." The man nodded as Arman and Dustin returned to their ride.

The man just stood in front of the fallen roadkill deciding on his next move, as the woman shouted at him repeatedly to get back in the truck. Arman had questions, he knew Dustin's parents hunted, but he just thought Dustin didn't. Many thoughts swirled around Arman's head. It was hard to picture Dustin as a hunter, someone willing to get blood on their hands. Arman's face made a look like he was puckering his sphincter.

Back in the car, Gary was busy getting the death stare from Arman as they sped off, while Amir wouldn't shut up about the encounter.

"I'm just saying, they acted weird is all. Like they were afraid Arman and I would mug them." Amir believed his, and to a lesser extent, Arman's opinions on the damage were not well received because of the color of their skin. "They were clearly uncomfortable because of how dark we are."

Jordon the ever-loving and rather naive boyfriend reassured Amir, only briefly looking up from his phone. "Babe, they didn't care how dark you are, they thought you guys were terrorists." Returning to his absent-minded scrolling. Clearly understood by his tone, everybody knew Jordon honestly believed he was helping.

"Ha, welcome to the bible belt... Mohammad!" Gary burst into self-righteous laughter.

"Screw you, Gary!" His bitterness spewed towards Gary, however, Amir's glare seethed towards Jordon.

Like all festering scabs, the bickering slowly dimmed to a throbbing sore griping here and there, then after far too long flecked off like dried blood and died. The last death rattles of whining blowing away like dust as the group stopped for gas, getting stares by more pasty white folks in the Big Haus station.

Pouring out of the car again at the last pit stop until the city, Gary left Dustin to fill the tank as he and Jordon hit the head, leaving Amir and Arman to pay and grab snacks for the road.

"Do you want anything?" Arman asked as Dustin grabbed the nozzle.

"Naw I'm good." He replied turning his attention to the darkness encircling the gas station.

Arman strolled into the convenient store along with Amir, self-conscious that their complexions were a few shades darker than any other person in the pale fluorescent lights. Normally at this time of night in the Midwest, the dudes aimlessly wandering the Big Haus like zombies, would snicker or make some sort of brazen insult letting the two men know how ignorant and frightfully stupid white folks are capable of being. Except for some reason the five or so pale males in the gas station appeared to be more worried and a bit creeped out by the lone man near the SUV.

Dustin stood at the edge between the light and the surrounding darkness. Literally, at the edge, the black of night encircled the radius of the station in a line, no diffused light blending into the night. Dustin stood simply watching an old friend go about its work, unperturbed by any hill jack or yammering lackwits in the place. He was relaxed and smiling, calm and serine knowing nobody would dare try anything against him or his traveling companions.

Occasionally the counter attendant thought he'd seen movement as Arman and Amir looked on just trying to get the transaction over with. Attempting to pay attention to the men attempting to pay for gas and snacks, the counter guy in some ugly cut off flannel shirt and ball cap kept looking over at Dustin in the lot.

"Did you see that?" Asking of Arman.

"See what?" speculating that the guy had done too much trucker speed.

Mumbling "nothing", the attendant would swear to his buds he'd seen jets of blackness streak through the lot. Like a fast-moving pack of wolves circling, moving closer with each second, darting in and slipping out as the man behind the counter cast his gaze around. Jutting at him if he looked away, a dark face out of the corner of the eye, the impending entropy or foreboding choking the air out of the man's lungs.

The guy behind the counter had some perception, a perception that made his friends tense, they had no time for Arman or Amir, all eyes were waiting for the oncoming darkness. As if the night was testing the defenses waiting to attack.

Making their way back to the vehicle Amir barked that the gas nozzle was still attached, "do I have to do everything himself." Gary and Jordon were in their seats looking annoyed. Upset it seemed Arman was taking too long to pay. They didn't like it there and wanted to be on the road ASAP.

"Get in already!" Gary cried out to Arman as he returned to the vehicle.

"Shut up, I'm waiting for Dustin." Snarking at his boyfriend, not the last time on the trip that would be happening.

"Uggghh!" Gary expelled.

Arman hesitated to get in the backseat, about to call to Dustin; watched as he again nodded his head, turned and walked back quickly to the car. He knew they'd forget he was even in the car and drive off until Arman smacked them into shape to make the guys come back for him. Outwardly calm and happy Dustin slipped into the backseat as an impatient Gary revved the engine.

"You alright?" Arman looked at Dustin sideways, smirking a little.

"Oh yeah, totally." Dustin had no need to fill his friend in at this point.

About to pull out of the lot and back onto the highway, they were cut off by a blue pickup swerving recklessly around them slamming its brakes on at the front entrance. Some random guy running inside.

Pissed he almost hit a second vehicle in one night Gary shouted "Asshole!" punching the wheel with his fist, then deciding to use his better judgment he peeled out of the lot in a rage-fueled huff. This wouldn't have been the best time to say anything so Arman and Amir kept quiet as Gary madly burned rubber down the road. Jordon puckered up and Dustin wasn't worried. So they all let the baby have his way and drive like a heedless dick for a few minutes. Behind them a few bright flashes were coming from inside the store, then as quickly the lights darkened and flickered.

A few miles down the way Gary had calmed down and the group could see lights glowing in the distance from the city. Traffic picked up on the highway and as they got ever closer Gary's mood perked up. He was surprisingly okay with a blue pickup barreling passed him, weaving dangerously between lanes to make top speed toward St. Louis. Under his breath, "someone's in a hurry" as the driver sped by.

"We should stop for the night." Arman peeped out from the back.

"It's still early, we should keep going." Gary was amped, he'd gotten his second wind.

"Past St. Louis there's nothing out there." Dustin spoke with quiet certainty.

"Then you'd better find us a place to stay." Gary directed his statement to Arman like Dustin hadn't said a word.

As they approached the city, Jordon and Amir were mostly quiet, Dustin completely, as Arman and Gary bickered over hotels, yes to some features no to others. Dustin didn't care that much, he'd have no real say in it anyway.

"Alright, I got us rooms." Arman called out, happy to be done dealing with it.

"Thank god, where?" Jordon was so happy to have a location to operate from.

"A bed and breakfast near downtown."

"Is it...?" Before Gary could rebuke Arman's booking he was cut off. His distrust was expected.

"Near a bunch of bars, yes. And it has a pool." Smugly rebutting his lover.

"Ha-ha. We'll never get Gary back on the road." Amir smirked.

"Funny, dick!" Gary didn't like the insinuation. "Just get a motel, we'll be leaving in the morning."

"The conference is days away. What's the point of driving if we can't stop along the way to enjoy?" Amir made a valid point. But only to annoy Gary.

"Fine, I could use a good night out anyway." Fidgeting about in his seat.

Unbeknownst to the other's, Gary and Jordon partook a little something in the restroom at the gas station, now he'd have to shift his focus from driving continuously for the next twenty-four hours to doing some light barhopping. He'd taken a gamble and it could go either way, however historically it would end badly for someone. Perhaps this time it would be Gary.

Focusing on his driving, Gary weaved and careened down the highway like a man with a death wish. He was intent on making it to their location, even if it killed everyone in the vehicle. No one seemed all that concerned, they had seen Gary like this more times than they could count, part of the trepidation about Gary driving in the first place. This would just be one more thing to mock him about later.

Making it into St. Louis roughly an hour later, they arrived at their temporary residence early enough to salvage the evening. Or so they hoped.

IV

After the torturous journey to St. Louis, the group gratefully piled out of the SUV in front of the Regent House. An early American federalist building renovated to be a sassy and brassy gay hotel and perhaps brothel. Well, that was the hope anyway for Gary, Jordon, and Amir. There was no indication it was anything other than a mildly tacky bed and breakfast. A small family-run hotel trying to compete with the corporate giant's type of establishment. Moderately clean, nicely decorated and had a very calming lobby after a long road trip.

Grabbing the myriad of overnight bags Dustin and the fourgy, trekked to the front desk to encounter a bright-eyed, aging twink ready to welcome them with open arms. And if asked nicely, an open bed by the look on his face.

"Welcome, come on in! Don't be shy. I'm Brad, how can I help you?" Such a dandy middle American accent. All guttural without the twang. Charming enough if you lived there, but a bit taxing for these east coast travelers.

"Uh, hi. I booked online, like an hour ago or so." Arman stepped up, Dustin off to the side, scanning the lobby.

The floorplan was rather spacious, on the left by the check-in desk was the stairwell leading up to the rooms, at its base an adjacent dining room, now closed. On the right of the front entrance, there were a couple of puffy high backed fabric chairs and a table with advertisements for local businesses, some fag rags, and assorted bowls of condoms. The overall theme was chill and gave a casual vibe. Dustin thought *cool,* they're not trying to pretend to be super classy or anything.

"Name." All the pleasantries and such. The boring stuff.

"Arman Salah-Navuluri." By the face change on Brad, Arman's words became gibberish. Dustin smirked, unnoticed in the back.

"Um, okay... Sorry, I have it here." He wouldn't even try, *how sweet*. Better than all the teachers Dustin and Arman had growing up. "There was a problem with the booking."

"I knew it. We should've just kept driving." Huffing, Gary dropped his gym bag on the floor.

"No, it's fine. One of the rooms you booked had an issue, the bathroom is being cleaned." Waving his manicured nails around to reassure the weary travelers it was under control.

"So we have to squeeze into the other rooms?" Jordon puffed, not sounding thrilled like it would somehow cramp his style or something. Dustin like everyone else knew full well Jordon would only use the room to wipe away the filth as he prepared to go hustle for more green. How Amir could be so oblivious, *must be true love,* Dustin mused ironically.

"Room, I only booked two rooms."

"Two! Where's everyone going to sleep?" Gary fumed. Arman didn't appear to like his tone, responding accordingly.

"If you weren't being an ass all night, you would have known that! But you were too busy driving like a maniac. What with the weaving and the tapping... Seriously Gary; you were driving like you were going to run us into a ditch! You know... never mind." Making a zip-it movement with his index finger and thumb across Gary's snout.

Arman winked at Dustin, his way of informing his friend everything was fine. In the classic 'it would be fine' future sense, so Dustin shouldn't worry about a big fight between Gary and Arman. Dustin wasn't, in fact, he found this one of the odder aspects of Gary and Arman's relationship. Having to challenge each other for some sort of foothold in their hierarchy of dominance. While Dustin found it fascinating to dissect the flaws and foibles of Arman's relationship, for purely academic purposes, he thought perhaps he should feel saddened that his friend hadn't yet realized he deserved better.

In time perhaps, Dustin thought. This trip was promised to unveil and unravel the threads that bound Dustin's 'friends' to their old lives. Bringing them was a big reason he agreed to make the trip home in the first place. Otherwise, his mom would focus on him, making any journey home abysmal and pointless. Dustin would much rather be hunkered down poolside somewhere far away on his summer break, bravely hiding from his mother.

"It's alright, one room has almost been cleaned..."

"Fine, Amir and I will take the one that's ready, Gary can wait." Looking directly at the front desk person instead of his phone, Jordon made a frustrated, almost impatient expression, like he was behind schedule for some such thing.

"Hold on. Arman booked it, so we get first dibs!" Turning frustration back on Jordon. Gary twitching slightly, wanted to be out and about partying, not stuck in a lobby of some dumpy hotel.

"You guys don't get to decide anything." Arman was about to take out his earrings for a knockdown bitch fight, but thankfully Brad interrupted.

"The other room has an odor. So..."

"You guys take it." Gary volunteering it to Amir.

Arman put his hand up, silencing them. The attendant wasn't finished, he wanted to see what was going on before they got kicked out for fighting and had to go find another place to stay. Dustin watched Arman's temple pulse, he knew he was keen on using the nuclear option, but wanted a tad bit more intel before he went ballistic.

"Sorry, you were saying?" All charming like, making a big fake smile. Not sure exactly who to become angry at yet, however wearing a veneer of smiles that could turn cold and murderous any second, Arman breathed, waiting for his answer.

"We had a last minute cancellation. I took the liberty of moving you to the lover's suite. It's two rooms, joined by a central bathing area. It's our best room." Brad had a gaze that came off like prurient interest meets killer clown causing a car wreck. Dustin found his expressions to be so vivid he could read his thoughts simply by his face.

"That sounds great, thank you." Arman sounding like a happy camper again. Except, then there was Gary to change that.

"What about Dustin?"

"What about him? He's staying in our room, there's two beds..." Turning to Brad for clarification. "There are two beds, right?"

"Yes, in the secondary room there are two, in the main suite there's one large bed." Smiling to appease the irritated guy with the long last name.

"We'll take the single." Jordon volunteered the space like he owned it. Amir perked up, grinning broadly, but only for a moment. "You guys have it settled then? Great, I need the keys." a cursory glance at Arman, then to Gary. Jordon wanted to get moving.

"Why do you need the keys?" Gary clutching them tightly.

"I've got an appointment."

"No. You promised no work this week." Disappointment washed over Amir's mug.

"Sweetness, it's fine, I promise." He pulled Amir close, and with his seductive charms soothed his lover. "It's just a massage, the tables in the car. Nothing more."

"No. Please don't go."

"We need the money." The lie evident in his tone.

"Fine, just a massage. Nothing else." And over Amir's head apparently. Dustin shook his.

"I promise." Pecking Amir on the lips.

"Well, if you're going, drop us at a bar." Gary tossed the keys to Jordon, smiling now as Amir groveled.

"Fine, where do you want to go?" Jordon looked at Gary, who looked to Brad, past an angry Arman.

"There's the Showboat, it's in the central west end, that might be your crowd." Brad got a sneer from Arman.

"So, you're just going to split and leave us with this then?"

"You have it under control. Meet us there." He was so oblivious it was almost cute. Almost. *There's that pulsing vein again*, Dustin mused to himself noticing Arman's temple.

Jordon pulled a still distraught Amir by the arm out the front with Gary, following behind them all sorts of happy. They acted without a thought given to Arman being left to deal with the bags. Even less thought than that (if that was possible) given to how Dustin would react. To them, he'd deal because that what he does. In their collective consciousness, Dustin was the guy who held the door, nothing more, nothing less.

"Asshole!" Turning back to the counter, Arman seethed.

"Um, sir. If it helps in any way, when the reservation was canceled, they had prepaid for a full bar and several gift selections. Mostly edibles that either need to be used or thrown out." The compassion and understanding in Brad's expression and tone sounded genuine.

"Full bar?" Perking up.

"Very. Full of premium liquor. It was supposed to be a second honeymoon for the couple, they went all out with the amenities."

"Really Brad... Tell me, why'd they cancel last minute like that? Especially if they already paid for everything." Dustin was now intrigued enough to engage in the back and forth. He'd simply been watching and absorbing all that transpired.

"I shouldn't say anything, but the gentleman who made the reservation, Ernie Hudson, was planning a surprise anniversary weekend for his husband Dabney. Well, they were going to have a bunch of friends and spend the weekend rekindling..." Spilling his guts like he just ate late-night sushi from a gas station.

"Um Brad, we don't need their life story, just what happened to cause the cancellation." Dustin spoke calmly and serenely. His voice washed over the front desk attendant like a soothing wave.

"Sorry, I get carried away, they've been coming here for years. Well, they had a major collision on the way here. Swerved off the road right into a tree. It happened earlier this evening. Their friends called us while we were dealing with the leak in the other room." He rambled.

"That's dreadful, and?" Dustin asked softly.

"Oh. Mister Hudson may not make it, and mister Newerth; his partner, is said to be in a medically induced coma. They're on death's door I'm afraid."

"Humph!" Dustin snorted a derisive laugh, shaking Brad out of his deeply concerned glare. "That, that's tragic. Just awful. And the leak?" Dustin got some serious side-eye from Arman over the snickering.

"About the time of the accident, the pipe just burst. We were so swamped, the preparations were all set and it was just a madhouse here. Luckily we have it under control now." Brad didn't have a look like it was all under control. In fact he stared at Dustin like he thought this guy was a cold hearted bitch for laughing at someone else's tragedy.

"Yeah, well it sounds like you guys really know what you're doing. I'm sure they'll be okay, don't worry yourself about it." Dustin was trying hard to keep a straight face. He wanted to laugh so badly and it was apparent to the other two men.

Attempting to subdue Brad's emotion and deflect the glares he was getting, Dustin made hand gestures trying to apologize. Failing that, turned to grab their bags. He didn't like the way they were looking at him, so best change the scene. *If only he could say something* but that, Dustin thought, would just make the situation stranger.

It did the trick though, like all was forgotten. Dustin, then Arman started collecting the bags, Brad scrambled to help them carry their luggage and the many overnight bags the other guys dumped off up the stairs to their suite. Arman stewed thinking, tossing Gary's gym bag up the stairs, kicking it down the hall when they got to the top. Dustin knew Arman well enough that if he was kicking Gary's toiletries, then he'd be starting to evaluate his relationship with the meat-sack. That wouldn't bode well for Gary, but it did take attention away from Dustin's guffaw at laughing at critically injured husbands on a second honeymoon.

V

After an appropriate time acclimating in the suite, consisting mostly of Dustin and Arman moving the bar cart from the main room to the one with the double beds, and stripping the main suite of all the luxury items they wanted to horde, pillows, fancy towels that sort of plunder, Arman was ready to open up and bitch about Gary. Frustrated before, but mostly tight-lipped, now he was ready to pop like a Mormon's cherry. With a few drinks behind him, he spewed some rather hateful insults he'd been saving to really get under Gary's skin. Dustin just sat casually enjoying a cocktail while letting Arman get it all out of his system.

This was one more aspect he couldn't understand about interpersonal relationships. Withholding information on how you feel. Especially if your upset. As far as Dustin was concerned he should be screaming at Gary and not at his drink. The whiskey didn't hurt his feelings after all. But Arman wouldn't do that unless he was pushed to his limit.

Dustin and his family, they had many secrets, but when it came to interpersonal relationships, they shared everything. Most outsiders and to a large extent Dustin believed there was far too much sharing. Dustin only felt that way because growing up, he had a chance to see how Arman's family behaved and found it surreal. How they held back from telling each other important things; like when they were angry about something. Or how they acted like everything was alright even when clearly a situation was a disaster. It was so dysfunctional for Dustin he couldn't get enough. The flipside was Arman always wanted to be around Dustin's family, a place where secrets were pried loose like the casing on a coffin. And truths were dug up like a body to be picked apart the way cadavers used to be for medical research.

After a time, with Arman calm and chipper again the two set out to salvage the remainder of their night with the fellas. Arman always felt

Dustin was good to bounce ideas off of, and in times of stress, like the present, to give helpful advice. Arman having vented could now talk to Dustin in a rational tone to get some clarity over his relationship. Dustin would as per usual, stay calm and collected, he had other things on his mind, but would listen and be helpful in his way to soothe his annoyed friend. A friend who was acting like he was attempting to find some reason not to dump Gary's lame ass. A reason Dustin knew didn't exist, so he would; without being judgmental at all, find a way to convince Arman to drop Gary like a body from a bridge.

"It's so infuriating! He, all of them actually, acting like I didn't matter and wasn't even there! I really hate it..." This was not a common feeling for Arman, so he was a bit bent out of shape over it all.

"I don't believe Gary saw it that way. In his weird way, he's trying to show you he's a big boy." Dustin knew this situation all too well, it happened to him daily. So why, he thought, get all worked up over it. Plus, when push came to shove, Gary was a tool.

"I don't know how, but okay." Not sure how his friend got to that rationale. "But honestly. They act like you don't matter. Or worse, aren't even there most of the time. How is it you're so calm about it?"

"That's not true." Getting the stink eye. "I exist when they need something." Dustin smirked, this was no big to him so seeing Arman all upset about it was a little bit funny.

"See, you're making jokes, I'm serious Dustin. I know how they treat you and it sucks."

"Arman, people are just the way they are. You can't really change them, only yourself. I don't get worked up over it because that's who they are. Gary, for example, is just being true to his nature."

"What's Gary's true nature, an ass?"

"Most of the time sure. He's trying to act like an alpha male, they all are. Gary wants to prove to you he can take charge and be strong because deep down he doesn't feel he's good enough to be with you."

"I'm not sure I agree, but either way that's too profound for this hour."

Really, it's true. It's also true he's not good enough for you. Or for that matter, not good enough to be allowed in public most of the time."

"True that."

"Look, Gary loves you, about as much as he can love anybody. He's desperate to prove it, which causes him to act out like a four-year-old."

"That actually does sound like him, which sucks because I just wanted a boyfriend, not a child. Maybe a boyfriend I could have children with, but not that, and probably not him." Looking at Dustin with sincere respect.

"Look, give it some time before you dump him. Tell him to get his act together and grow up, and this is how it has to be. He's not the brightest after all." Dustin was still super casual about it, taking in the broader scenery. "Also it'd be a downer with him pouting the rest of the trip. He's such a baby!"

Arman chuckled. "I'll try."

"When we get to Santa Fe you can kick him to the curb, how bout that?" Smiling. Something was drawing Dustin's attention closer.

"I like that plan. So, have any of them even thanked you for getting us an all-expenses paid vacation?"

"You did, but you don't have to, and it's not me anyone should thank. Mom knows you appreciate it."

"But still, I know your parents are awesome, but to pay for the five of us to come out and spend a week in New Mexico, that takes the cake."

"Not really, Nate's got his plans, Marta's up to something, and frankly as the organizer of this interfaith thing, she's using her connections as a write off for the business."

"Come on, even you have to admit you have the coolest parents ever."

"Well Marta and Nate appreciate that, and they think you're pretty spiffy as well."

"Thank you?" Giving Dustin a sideways glare. The side of his mouth turned up.

"Look, I don't want to think about my parents until we get there."

"Why? What did you do?"

"I have no idea what you're talking about." Faining ignorance.

"Please, I've known you forever, your being tightlipped about something. What are you hiding from them?" Arman's steely gaze staring at Dustin. "I thought something was up with you, now I know it's about your parents."

"It's not about them, but you know how my mom is, if I mention anything she knows."

"Yeah it's creepy, I still think she put a bug on you, but it's just us, no one else. What are you hiding? And why?"

"Fine. You can't say anything to anyone, not until I decide what to do. Agreed?" Arman nodded his agreement. "I'm not going back this year, I'm thinking of hitting the road."

Arman stopped in his tracks, mouth opened. "What? Why, why would you just bail on that gig?" Meaning Dustin's rather cushy job.

"I was let go. The college is shutting down the ethnographic studies department."

"Why, you just published that book. You have that theory that makes total sense, I think? You're an asset to the school."

"Well, thank you. But seriously, it's not going to be a best seller or anything. It's an academic piece. And my theory can't be proven."

"You just need to go on an expedition or something, find the evidence and show them you're right about that whole origin of species thing."

"Really? Did you read the copy I gave you... any of it?"

"I read a lot." Getting a rather stern glare. "Okay, some." A deeper stare. "Fine, like fourteen pages, and I skimmed the pictures."

"Not including the introduction?"

"Like seven pages; mostly... Plus the pictures. Thank you for the shout out by the way."

"You're welcome." Coming off a little flat, he'd hoped Arman would make it a bit further into it.

"Sorry, it's just that I don't really understand most of what you were talking about."

"Neither did the college. I proposed doing research abroad, but they're right when they said it can't be proven." Sighing, Dustin lamented. "After a certain point, unless there's some magical Rosetta stone or a picture taken by aliens, you can only definitively follow folklore back through to the origin of written language."

"That part I get, but why not? What about those cave paintings and stuff?"

"That's evidence but what it means is speculative. There's no quantifiable way of determining if a single individual or a group of sapiens became sentient. Or when or if, it was limited to one species, or spread out to many sapien species and because folkloric traditions were handed down orally, there is no clear proof to find the specific origination of any particular belief system."

"Yeah." Arman nodded his head, with that lovely blank stare. "And that's where I get lost. But there's got to be something you can do? You could maybe..."

Arman continued to talk as Dustin's attention shifted elsewhere. Like a wave, Dustin felt the world shift. As if a storm was about to break, the air became electric. That feeling of energy bustling, now consuming the visual spectrum around him. They were being led somewhere by a thing in the night. A cold sensual tingle ran down Dustin's spine as Arman droned on.

Dustin let his thoughts drift into it. The intensity of the apparition was coming closer as the night passed, but why after all this time, he pondered. Maybe a burden lifted? Maybe to see the other one as he moved about. More likely it was that Dustin, for the first time in years was at an impasse in his life where he could stop and see creation in a new light. Not bogged down by study or work, he was at a crossroads, and it was likely the darkness now wanted him in their crosshairs.

The ground resonated with waves of light. An ethereal pale blue rippling and popping all around. Tiny sparks and flares bursting about, in the trees, the sky, along the ground. Bits of bacteria coming to life, a chick just hatched from an egg, flies and mosquito's emerging to take their place in this ecosystem.

Interspersed among this new life, along the grass and concrete, the tree-lined streets with their houses, a host of wonders all being born in these moments. New molds and single-celled organisms. Larger creatures coming in to the world in the shadows between houses, the walls, and rooms of buildings. A new litter of puppies born in an alley, Dustin could see all of this blue azure light ebbing and flowing like pulse waves in the spectrum, he was seeing life in its waveform.

It was a simple matter of adjusting to this new sensory world before there was the flip side. The death that came, life extinguished in black waves, sparking and popping in flares and busts. One of the puppies snuffed out, a mouse being eaten by a hawk, the flies that lived dying, bacteria and fungus evaporating as if they never existed. Dustin knew he was there, he was showing himself in the blackness. Not in his full form, but Dustin knew there was a smile, a cheeky grin teasing and playing in the darkness.

That's why he was seeing this. He wanted Dustin too. He was, in fact, leading Dustin, and by extension Arman right to where he would show himself again in person. Or at least a person of sorts. A visible representation of a person.

"Well, you could always take your book on tour. Do the lecture circuit." Arman had gotten to his point, a long way to go for simple advice, but there it was.

Dustin's focus was being pulled back to Arman, but before he returned to the real world his last thought on the stranger in the dark was, *why doesn't he just ask me out? Such a dork.*

"A lecture circus?" Back now.

"I said take it on a lecture circuit."

"Well, that makes more sense."

"I don't know. Now that I think about it, you could do readings from your book as part of a carnival."

"I could, I mean my field of expertise is about as rare as a sideshow. Maybe I will. The death rituals of early Neolithic nomadic peoples of the Ural Mountain range. I'll read it next to the sword swallower, that way people will stay awake."

"You're too hard on yourself. Although it sounds like a snooze fest, you deserve credit for being an expert in your field. Me, I just hope to land a job in mine."

"Ancient, archaic folklore, isn't the most sought after profession but thank you. And you will get a decent job, you always land on your feet."

"Still complimenting me, worried I'll tell your parents?"

"I am. I'm worried how they'll react."

"Really! They of all people would be supportive of you losing your job."

"That's not why I haven't told them. You know how they are, my mom would want me to move home and run the shop for her."

"Yeah, I get that. Do you think she suspects something's up and that's why she invited all of us?"

"You sound paranoid. Of course she is, and it was exactly why. I refused to say anything, so she wants to interrogate all of you."

"Ah, not the first time she's done that. Has your mom at least told you anything about where we're staying? We're not all going to fit in their guest room."

"You and I get to stay in the apartment above the store. Dad renovated it."

"That's cool. What about... Them?"

"You'll love this, dad and his men's group volunteered their yurt." Dustin made a shoot me in the head, mock smile.

"They have a yurt?" Arman made a face. The face he made every time he saw Dustin's dad, a nudist, walk into a room. It was an unhinged face.

"Yup, it's their sacred space to deal with all the masculine energy work. You know, so they're not so toxic."

"Oh, god! That sounds like it's going to smell like..."

"Old socks, sweat, and lube. With copious amounts of sage."

"Serves those assholes right!"

"Want to hear what's worse?" A glint of evil flashed across Dustin's eyes.

"Worse than your dad and his group of freaky friends? Oh, most definitely!"

"To show how supportive their men's group is with the LGBTQ community, they booked Jordon for a week of bodywork." The sinister flash in Dustin's eyes spread to an equally sinister smile.

"Does he know?" Mild shock and delight on Arman's pretty mug. This was too good to be true.

"Not yet, but you know how it is with Nate and Marta." The sinister faded into dismay.

"Yeah, when they want something it just happens. Which is odd, I've never been able to quite figure out how that works." A chill ran down Arman's spine, Dustin's parents had reputations growing up, strange ones.

"We've both tried and both failed. I haven't been able to hide anything from them since I went to Grandma Hester's that summer." Sighing.

"The one time you got in trouble in your life! Thirteen, and your punishment was to spend a blissful summer in the English countryside. You poor thing!" The sarcasm dripped from Arman's tongue.

"It was so rough." Dustin made a mock plea for pity. His fond memories of that trip couldn't be concealed. "I haven't answered any calls, or checked any texts, emails or letters in the last week." Dustin was content to stay in the dark if only to keep his parents in the dark.

"Now you're sounding paranoid. Letters? Not even a bill, or junk mail?" Arman eyeballed him like he was some crazy little man out very far on a limb. A limb that was about to break.

"No social media and I haven't checked my mail, period. I'm not being paranoid, remember when you opened your locker on our last day of school, the raven?" Meeting suspicious eyes with a determined stare. "I don't need anymore strange animals on my doorstep right now."

Arman's eyes flashed wide. "Oh my god, I almost shit myself! It just stood there holding the invite to your graduation party."

"Yeah, the party we didn't know I was having. You had it easy, that sort of stuff is what my parents do, and Marta has been stepping it up since I went silent. I just need time to decide what I want to do." Not as calm as before, Dustin was riled by his mother breathing down his neck.

"Look I get it, you don't have to justify it to me. Your parents may be nuts, but they're still really cool." Arman wanted to sooth Dustin but still managed to gush over how cool he thought Dustin's parents were. "I mean that party was so amazing. Your dad hosting a kegger for our graduation. DJ, full bar, and those party favors. Remember?"

"Thanks to those party favors, not really."

"How they didn't get arrested for serving a truck ton of booze to high school kids is beyond me." Arman gave up trying to figure that out years before.

"Maybe it was all the dirt they got on everyone from the Memorial Day barbeque... The entire school board drunk at a naked pool party. I still get shivers." They each made a poo face, Dustin had to push that memory out of his mind as soon as he said it. "That's where you lucked out in the parent department. I grew up with all that. I can't unsee any of the countless number of times I walked into the den, with those groups of people spread out on our sofa."

"Who knew Scranton had so many nudists?" Trying to vanquish the images.

"I did, that's what I mean. I would have loved some of the boundaries, or any of the privacy you had." Dustin made a pouty, *feel bad for me* face. It was only somewhat effective. Arman was sort of immune to that ploy.

"Yeah, I get that. Like when your mom tried to hook you up with, what was his name? The smelly hippy, the blond one, with that knit sweater?"

"Oh him... That random, Sunbow. Not sunbeam... Not rainbow, but Sunbow. How is it, someone with a name like that, would be so averse to personal hygiene. No amount of patchouli makes up for not showering! Thankfully Marta made him leave. I swear she picks up these strays, tries to fix them and when that doesn't work, she dumps them off on the side of the road where she found them."

"At least he slept outside most of the time. It took me a month to get the smell out of my clothes."

"I threw my clothes away."

"I was grounded for months, my parents thought I was smoking dope."

"You were. At my house, with my parents." Dustin raised his brow to Arman. "And you weren't grounded for months, it was like a week; at most.

"True, but both my parents work and didn't want me at home by myself. You might have hated it, but they were fun times." At this point, all hope of sympathy for Dustin was gone.

"My parents work. Mostly from home, so they were always in my business. I would have loved to be grounded at your house."

"There's no way my mom would ever leave you alone in our house. You would have had every animal in the neighborhood in the living room." Arman sneered playfully at Dustin. "Better to leave them at your house."

"We didn't have every animal in the neighborhood at my house, just a couple of pets." Sneering back, less playfully.

"Pets? The crows and ravens? How many cats were there; like fifty?" Dustin scoffed at the notion, as Arman continued on. "The rabbits. Spiders, lots of spiders. God knows why? Lizards, turtles, frogs and all the other things... What was with the frogs?" Fond yet extremely odd memories for Arman.

"There was only one frog in the house, the rest were toads. And most of those weren't my pets. Just the one cat." Sticking his tongue out at Arman.

Laughing at Dustin, Arman began to reminisce as they walked, on the shenanigan's they got into growing up. Every bit of trouble any normal kid would have gone to juvie for, he and Dustin miraculously got away with. Just simple and fun little pranks and joy rides, in cars that may or may not have belonged to several members of the police department.

A few minor, harmless felonies along the way from childhood to adulthood. From breaking into their school to "accidentally" vandalizing the vehicles of the local bigots, it was just kid stuff. Those were the days. Arman was so glad they never got caught, Dustin however never entertained the thought of being caught. He knew better.

Coming up on the Showboat, their back and forth bantering quieted as Dustin and Arman got out their I.D.'s all prepared to pass them over the doorperson. A massive brick of a man, bald, built like a rather large bull wearing glasses, this guy in black was very intimidating to the two small men walking past. The meat-slab just waved them on, carrying on with his chums about the latest happenings in the 'scene'. The chit chat the bar crowd spew when things are dull.

The exterior of the building was an uninteresting blend of old family steakhouse meets VFW hall. A brick facade, interlaced with large concrete pots for assorted shrubbery, and slinky string lighting roped over a somewhat contemporary awning. As they entered it had that feel of a newly redecorated interior, ringing out with its hipster artist charms. Not a bad look by any means, a well reclaimed multi-use space much like large parts of the city. The lighting was set for a steamy, cruisy bar atmosphere. Backlighting with reds spots pulsing here and there. Small whiffs of fog steamed across the floor with folks dancing around in the corners.

In daylight, it might look somewhat classy with the dark paneled wood on every surface. But in the middle of this cluster of bodies in motion, looking to meet other bodies, for some motion: The look was dark lacquered black and a bit grungy. So, of course, Gary stood out like a sore thumb. Not that he was classy in any way, just that he'd put on his tightest white vee neck short sleeve to show off his rippling body and rock hard nipples.

Arman made that face he made each and every time he contemplated leaving Gary. The one where he was frustrated because he'd have to divide up their stuff. The face he'd been making so many times on this trip, and there it was again, now with the forehead vein popping out.

Gary wasn't alone. Thus, the reason for the angry vein reemerging on Arman's otherwise pristine mug. Dustin shook his head, he'd just managed to get Arman to calm that pulsating vein down, now it was going again at full strength. If Gary didn't stop acting like a major dick, Dustin believed, he'd soon be Arman's ex. The man who would be exiled alone in the middle of a city he wouldn't survive more than a day in, currently had his beefy arms around the waists of two very young men, draped and dripping off of him like ooze from a wound.

These "skank whore's", Arman mumbling inaudibly due to the loud rhythmic beats resonating through the establishment; had their collective arms on Gary's chest, thigh, and midsection moving down to the sweet spot. He was being rubbed down by twinks in tight clothing and Gary's excitement was getting more excited by the second.

Arman ponied up in front of the muscular man whom he shared a bed with. The man who was doing nothing to stop some random guy with bangs and *an unsightly sleeveless, midriff band shirt*; move his skinny paws along the inner waistband to reach for the kosher sausage with its cream-filled contents.

The other dude, with equally bad hair, puffy and sort of wavy; was stroking Gary's short shaved hair. Thankfully this boney boytoy had sleeves. Wearing a dark purple shirt, his belly exposed, with the man in the middle taking advantage of that. Using the exposed skin as consent to molest this dudes hip bones and crotch with his frisky paw. Dustin's stomach was beginning to flip watching this unsightly mess of bad clothing and even worse behavior. He felt terrible for Arman having to clean up that dripping tackiness. "Not enough disinfectant in the world..." Dismayed, rumbling under his breath.

Arman's ranker more than anything, rose much like his volume, by the sheer willingness to toss aside their at times, troubled relationship "for the first set of children who pay any attention to you. You half-baked daddy wannabe!" Arman's voice now shouting louder, each word hitting Gary's ear like a sharp edged ice pick.

He got caught; unaware it seemed, Arman was even in the bar. He'd planned on being finished long before his partner made it to the location by the dumbstruck look on his face. Finished with what exactly, Dustin didn't want to ponder, but it had something to do with busting his nut-sack. "ew..." Dustin vocalized, unable to keep his distain confined.

"Sweetie, babe! You got here quick..." Looking away from the purple shirts nipple and into Arman's seething gaze.

"Yeah, lucky us!" Taking a gander at the two boys entangled with his mate, then back to Gary with a greater sneer of hatred. "I see you found some new friends."

The arm candy glowered at Arman, wide eyed with wonder and licking their lips for some reason. Probably something gross and possibly contagious. They found Arman to be interesting apparently, so changed their expressions from sneers to pretty pouty puckers from what Dustin could see. He then wished for sudden blindness, so he wouldn't have to watch this derailing train about to crash into a station block.

"Um, yeah, these guys are a couple of locals I met, Axle and Townsend." Nodding to sleeveless first, it made sense, the name fit in a way. Then nodding to big-haired, purple shirt. Dustin now wanted someone to stab his ear drums, this was going to get as ugly, as the two twinks molesting Gary.

That's where Arman was reaching critical mass. Gary hadn't bothered removing his hands from either man's pants region. One hand on Axle's ass, now visible because the kid rubbed his loins against Gary. The other hand holding tight to the skin at the base of Townsend's cock. Pubic hair in between the fingers, very visible, thanks to the skimpy clothes.

Arman could no doubt see the dilation in Gary's wide eyes, because Dustin, who was currently standing back from the dribbling blast radius, could see it. More obvious was the sweat on the neckline and pits seeping down.

"You're high! We're going to get drinks, get rid of them before I come back!" Arman belched out in Gary's face. Spittle hitting the man now in shock.

"Yo bitch: You his boss? Back off!" In such a brassy tone it hit the ear with a twinge of pain.

From a really fucked up sounding dude *named after a car part*. Dustin sneered, edging closer. If need be, he'd intervene and then it would get uglier and that would be difficult cause he thought this guy was about as ugly as it got.

"Screw you, I'm his partner, or at least I was." More directed at Gary than Axle, Gary slipped off and out of the guys, attempting to pull it together.

He heard something in the tone of Arman's voice that tolled the bell on their relationship. The death knell on any chance at a life together, the same tone anyone within ten feet of the couple heard. Dustin on his worst day, could have understood what Arman meant, Gary was road kill in their life together. He'd messed up big time, and yet the truth was only just beginning to dawn on the dimmest bulb of the bunch. "Babe! I uh ..."

"Just shut it! Come on Dustin." Arman stormed away to the bar, fully intending to watch Gary crash and burn.

As he moseyed past Gary and the douche twins, Dustin paused to ask, "Where's Amir?" they may be leaving in a hurry so best keep tabs on everyone.

"Patio." Was all Gary could say, with his eyes though, he begged to enlist Dustin's aid in some way. *Stands to reason,* Dustin knew he'd only acknowledge him when he needed help, so he kept walking.

Arman was at the bar and had already gotten the attention of the bartender. *He'd only been at the bar, for like a second,* Dustin couldn't imagine that kind of attention, or why Gary could be so thick to let Arman slip away. Gary had, had it really good, and now just washed it all down the toilet like a prom night baby.

Within a minute or so, the dirty blond bartender passed Arman his drinks, he was about to pass off a vodka tonic to Dustin, *so thoughtful,* when yet another random dude slid right up in the middle of the two men. Dustin should have been more spatially aware, however, the hairs on his neck began tingling as he approached Arman. Someone had indeed lured them to this location, "sneaky monkey."

Arman never checked for directions to the bar where his now doomed boyfriend was getting handsy with the local tweakers. He relied on Dustin to navigate because he'd always relied on Dustin's innate ability to always know where he was going. Dustin generally just trusted the universe to steer, but he never told Arman that.

Either way they usually ended up where they needed to be. As he and Arman chatted on and on, Dustin allowed the other to take over and lead them on their merry way, getting them safely to the Showboat just in the nick of time. Before Arman would have caught Gary getting his ballsack deep-throated by a guy in a sleeveless midriff. That would have been so tacky. *A sleeveless midriff! Of all things*, Dustin shivered at the thought.

The individual butting his broad shoulders inbetween the two friends dispensed with the pleasantries by jumping straight over them. He was a shark circling its prey and really wanted to feast on Arman. This tall muscular, yet beefy dude had a black on black matching shirt pants combo, dark hair and an alright face. Alright in that Dustin didn't get a great look at it as he kind of got scooted out of the way so the meat-bag could make his move. Poor guy would never stand a chance, Arman hated the idea of sex or cheap pick up lines when he was angry, the guy had a flat ass so that was strike two and he just dissed Dustin which would surely bring out some misplaced ire.

"I couldn't help notice what happened back there." All smooth and sensual sounding in a sultry baritone.

"Excuse me…" Arman said, acting a bit surprised such a sultry voice came out of such a piece of garbage.

"That guy, back there. He's blind not to see how special you are." Leaning in a bit closer than necessary. "Let me buy you a drink. You shouldn't be by yourself." The smell of gin and desperation wafting in Arman's face. It was fairly strong, even Dustin could smell it, and the guy had his back turned in cock block fashion.

Making a face like he just threw up in his mouth, Arman responded as politely as a cobra would right before it strikes. "I have a drink. Two in fact, because I'm not alone. You'd know that if you weren't such a rude piece of trash." His tone was like stabbing the guy in the face with broken glass.

Arman moved around the guy slugging back as much of his Jack as he could in one gulp, handing Dustin his vodka. "I'm gonna hit the head." Talking with a full mouth.

Dustin sipped his drink as the bigger guy starred down at him. The intruder seemed stunned he'd been passed over for some forgettable man. Dustin didn't have to look at the guy to know the gears would be squeaking away. Formulating a plan to regain some of his manhood, like that even mattered.

Besides, Dustin had a more interesting view fade into the bar near him. The billowy shadow from the roadside earlier in the evening returned. Gossamer filaments of blackness wafted and rippled like sheer fabric in flowing water, this phantom wisped slowly by, keeping his smirking brow and onyx gaze on the corporeal mortal smiling at the bar.

"I didn't know, sorry. How are you doing?" Apparently, black pants on black shirt tried his hand at making small talk and had formed a plan. Try to impress Dustin, to get to Arman.

"Ha!" Dustin chuckled into his drink, his attention was elsewhere.

The apparition's slate blue and charcoal gray hands gestured him to follow. He was heading towards the restrooms. Arman wasn't the intended so Dustin set his drink down, ignored the chattering dude and casually walked to the men's room.

Inside it was as if Arman hadn't missed a beat, he picked up on the thought he wanted to convey and ran with it the moment Dustin was near.

"Can you believe the nerve! What complete pigs. First, Gary hooking up with the street trash, and that guy at the bar, acting like

I need rescue and that you don't exist!" Arman was angry alright, he wanted to vent but was blocked, so now that Dustin was present, the flood gates gushed. Thankfully his body already gushed and was zipping up, heading over to wash his hands.

Absentmindedly "um hmm" coming from Dustin as Arman rambled, Dustin watched the spectre try again to impress him. The apparition phased through the last bathroom stall escorting a scared translucent figure into the main area of the restroom. It's bone hand on one shoulder leading in dead guy out past the living. The poor soul looked like a ghost. Actually, a ghost of a ghost, of its former self. Paler, more so than a pale translucent figure moving past Dustin would usually look in this situation. Its eyes hollow and circled with dark rings, waxed over. Its face so sad and lost looking.

The spirits shape, thin and bruised, with many visible track marks across its semi-transparent form. Ratty stained clothes thankfully added in their noncorporeal form. An illusion to give the dead some modesty. They weren't much help. The lingering thought of its garments showed how bad off this man was in life, now reflected in death. *Poor soul* Dustin lamented.

The tall spirit in its black shroud tightly gripped its boney hand on the shoulder of the dead soul, so it wouldn't try to flee. This person who was no more, appeared to be terrified and shaking. Powder stains under the nose, an ethereal outline of a bag on the shirt-line, with white dust on the hands from snorting. The spectre escorting the dead guy had his sympathetic sad frown on, but stone silent as he moved slowly passed Dustin. It turned, so Dustin did as well, maintaining eye contact.

The shroud reached out its arm like extension, touching Dustin on the cheek, then as it floated passed, ran its skeletal hand down Dustin's arm to his outstretched hand. As the black gaseous form floated by a little dance between Dustin and the spirit happened, both twirling slowly, eyes locked and a visible smile on Dustin's face. The corpse and Arman just pieces in a greater game, a game of flirtation.

This seductive dance of slow turns and timid hands touching tentatively gave Dustin ample time to see the spirit of the man who just died. Its physical body still warm in the last stall, and sadly; the saddest thing to Dustin, wasn't the dying, but the pain and suffering this person brought upon themselves. This person now haunted with their own ghosts, until such time, he could find some absolution.

That and that, this guy, died alone in a bathroom stall from a drug overdose. In a bad metal band tee shirt. Like *really bad, nineteen-eighties, hair band kind of bad* shirt. Stained and with holes, it was well worn, which kind of meant this corpse liked this band or something. Dirty pale grey, chipped screen printed yellow lettering, with flecks missing of the big-haired quartet, in the ugliest clothes from the era. Dustin about cringed at the sight.

"Hello again." Their hands finally separating. Dustin now completely facing away from Arman, speaking to an invisible force. "I'd wish him to go with grace, but too late for that." Making a scrunchy face. "Good to see you though." Waving slowly at the phantom, who waved back as it faded from this reality.

"What?" Wondering why, then what and who exactly, Dustin was talking about or to. Arman with his wet hands, stared blankly at Dustin to see him talk and wave to nothing and no one. At least no one he could see. "What are you doing? Who are you talking to?"

Arman understood that Dustin may have been under some pressure, but wouldn't have believed, couldn't believe him to have gone mad, or have any kind of meltdown.

"Oh, nothing." Playing off being caught acting like a dewy eyed child as best he could.

Murmuring under his breath "it's always the quiet ones to watch out for." Half heartedly and only slightly seriously, Dustin heard, a tad annoyed.

"Di. Da... What's, the... What's that supposed to mean? I haven't done anything."

"Relax princess... I know your not crazy, it's you were just talking to someone who isn't here." Doing a three sixty, arms out.

Dustin blushing. "Sorry, I was just talking to an old friend." He got caught and decided why hide it. After all, there was the body to contend with.

"Okay? Who, we're the only ones in here unless someone came in and I missed it?" Arman glared "And what's this go with grace? Who, whose Grace, go where... Are you alright?" Arman's mouth was hanging open. If he left it like that for too long flies would make a nice home of it.

"I'm fine. I was talking to someone about the dead guy from the last stall... Oh, there's a dead guy in the last stall." Thinking, it probably would help Arman if the situation was put in context.

Arman's face froze. The look of shock and confusion was so endearing and precious. "What? Are you sure you're okay?" His words were very measured.

"Yeah, go look. He's still warm. Overdose, by the signs." Still smiling absentmindedly, Dustin flapped his hand limply toward the closed door of the stall.

Arman, with one eye on Dustin the other on the metal door, backed up and over to take a look. Dustin understood the apprehension, this wasn't the first time a person reacted like this. Once at the stall door, Arman pushed at it, but it didn't budge, just clanked.

"It's locked." Instinctively he dropped his voice to a whisper. "I think someone's in there."

"I know. He's not getting up." Dustin thought this conversation hopped a train and took it out to left field, in the next county over, so why not let Arman in and see where it implodes.

Arman peeked under the door to see legs sprawled out, the figure was wearing some fairly beat up black boots. "He's not moving."

"Yeah, he's dead. It's safe to look, he's not going to bite you." Dustin was completely unphased about the corpse in the stall, much to

Arman's chagrin. "He's got disheveled hair, like brown paper bag brown, a baggy of powder in his lap, and an awful tee from that hideous metal band Pythia." Dustin shook his shoulders in horrified disbelief.

Arman reached up to peek over, slowly moving to crane his head to take in the spectacle. "Like one Alyssa had when we were young?"

"This one's grey, same cover pic though." Dustin decided to take a moment and wash up.

"What a horrible band. I hated them, I was so glad she grew out of it."

"That's what happens when the teens hit the puberty." Mocking a parental tone. "I think it's hysterical how your dad used your sister's old band tees as cleaning rags. With her taste in music, it was about all they were good for." Dustin rolled his eyes and smirked.

"You know how he hated to waste money, too bad he did, some of that shit is nostalgic, even worth something these days." Arman was hedging at looking over, the small talk was helping.

"Your dad was doing the world a service. None of those big hair bands need to make a comeback, even if it's supposed to be ironic." Wiping his hands on a paper towel.

Arman was now distracted enough to peek over. Looking down he saw the dead guy, limp sagging arms, and that face. So gaunt and pale, with deep glassy eyes blankly staring out into the void. Arman rushed backward and pushed up against the wall. This was new and completely frightening for him. Not knowing what to do, or how to cope, he looked to Dustin for aid. Arman looked like he believed Dustin should be at least a little upset by these events. "There's a dead body in there." As if this was new news. "And you're standing there all ho-hum, and calm?"

"I know, it's not that big of a deal. We should probably get the guys and go. You know, before someone finds him." Dustin casually turned to walk out the door. He knew Arman would follow.

Whispering, badly. "We're just going to leave him, shouldn't we do something?" Arman was afraid they'd be caught, or get into trouble or, who knew?

"We'll tell the door guy on the way out. I just don't want to stick around and watch everyone get all fussy over it. He overdosed, it wasn't like he was murdered." Dustin strolled on out to the bar, the music and lighting hadn't changed at all. Still loud and still annoying.

Arman followed, searching, scanning the room for Gary wanting a familiar presence and Dustin wasn't a very familiar person right then. The thought of the man, who may or may not become Arman's ex, caused something to click in his brain.

"Gary's fucked up on something." Trying to convey what he thought was important information.

"Yeah I know. We need to see where he got his shit and get him and Amir out before they cause a panic, so best to not make a scene. He's over there." Dustin pointed to Gary off alone in the corner. Looking sweaty and sad.

Arman paced up to Gary molesting his dripping head, checking for what Gary could only imagine to be ticks. Pawing and cupping his eyes and pulling his cheeks, Arman was in fact making a bigger scene than he'd just been asked not to make.

"You're high..." Barking loudly at Gary then focusing his attention to Dustin. "He's high, what do we do?" Arman was beginning to panic, Dustin took a breath remembering this was the first dead body for Arman, so he'd need to be patient with him.

"Babe, what's going on?" Swatting Arman's hands from his face. "I'm fine, really!" Gary didn't sound fine. A bit scratchy panic in his modulation. Made worse by Arman manhandling his jowls.

Hands free from the sticky flesh and sweat covered, Arman thought perhaps to wipe them off on Gary's shirt. However, seeing as that was also covered in sweat, he grimaced and ended up wiping his hands on his pants. Glaring at Dustin, panic was taking over. Any minute Arman would lose it and break down unless Dustin stopped him from bottoming out. Dustin knew there was a joke there somewhere, but would let it pass for now.

"Gary, we're going to be leaving in a minute but before that I need to ask you something." Calm and casual sounding Dustin was attempting to ease Gary into submission. *Another joke for another time,* Dustin needed to remember these people considered death and the dying stuff as being serious.

"Where's the ho-bags, what'd they give you? Where'd they get it from?" Arman panicking barking much louder than needed. His shill wail heard over the terrible dub-step rhythm playing.

Dustin stepped up, this was in his wheelhouse. Feeling he'd better step it up "Gary, focus. Arman wants to know where you got the blow from. And is trying to ascertain, if the two kids you were fawning over, had anything to do with it." His voice was so clear it cut through the music as if it was stone silent in the room. Arman stopped immediately, looking in awe at Dustin. When Dustin spoke both Gary and Arman knew he must be obeyed. Dustin, now the center of their universe was the calm and serene point where tranquility and obedience intersected.

"Townsend gave it to me."

By his expression Gary was more than a little bit scared of Dustin at the moment. Internally Dustin chuckled, thinking if he should make Gary wet himself in public. *Perhaps next time,* this was supposed to be serious, so he decided to stay focused on the task at hand.

"Do you know where he got it from, or from whom?" The words ringing in Gary's ear. Memories and insignificant details welled up, his thoughts opening like a lotus flower. Gary, if asked by Dustin, and only Dustin could recall all the sights, sounds and smells from everything he'd witnessed in the last day.

"Axle was talking to a man in the corner. The guy passed him a small white bag, Townsend pawned him a twenty."

"Describe the man who handed over the bag." Arman shocked, not having seen this side of Dustin before could only stand there and watch.

This terrifyingly powerful side. This new side, after he described a corpse at thirty feet away behind a closed door. Standing quietly with a blank expression, Arman was seeing a side that he clearly couldn't fathom coming from Dustin. Gary grimaced, doing the beginnings of the pee-pee dance. Arman noticed and even with all the oddness couldn't help but smirk.

"Messy hair. A brown, dark brown, but he was in shadows. Pale skin, he was wearing a grey tee shirt, it had holes and some stains. Also a picture, the words Pythia on the front, with a group of young women I think..."

"That's fine. Good boy, where's Amir, we've got to leave." Dustin patted Gary on the chest releasing him. The music flooded back in and his brain got all fuzzy again.

"Patio, why? What happened? What's going on?" Gary was so stunned and confused, looking back and forth from Arman to Dustin and back. He was feeling like his head would explode.

"We'll tell you on the way out." Leading the pack, which Gary and Arman were unaccustomed to, Dustin headed out to the patio at the back of the bar to find Amir, being circled by the same two men as Gary fawned over. Axle and Townsend, like bad cartoon vultures were seducing Amir with promises of the old loose and easy.

That was, until a sneering Dustin walked directly to Amir, with an Angered Arman, and disgusted Gary in tow. It was getting late, and the two possibly clap infected slut boys had just found some easy pickings, only to lose their prey to "of course" the annoying friends.

"Shoo... Go on; get!" Dustin waved them off like crows picking at roadkill. With aggravated sighs they split, heading separate ways to find another mark for wanton debauchery. Leaving a visibly high Amir alone and utterly confused. Turning around to find why his playthings evaporated mid-sentence, Amir's expression went cold seeing Arman and Gary snickering at him.

"What?" Exasperated for sucking the joy from his fellatio interruptis.

"Were leaving." Gary jumping at the chance to ruin Amir's night.

"Why, I want to stay. You go, I'll get a cab." Flat tone covering Amir's rising irritation.

"It's serious, we're going, now." Dustin spoke up, not with the tone of dominance, but just by speaking. To Amir that, and that they turned and began walking to the front door, made him curious enough to follow.

Backtracking inside, weaving through the bar, the four men headed to the main entrance. Dustin needed to let the door guy know something was up in the potty, and more importantly he needed Arman to stay calm until they made it out.

That would be the challenge. Gary and Amir kept begging to know "what was happening" and "why did you need to know about the blow?"

"Shut it, just because... Amir, you need to wipe your face." Arman shoved his hand in Amir's face when he noticed some powder.

"What?"

"Ha-ha, you got chandeliers." Gary chuckled.

"Shut it, that doesn't even make sense... Who says that anymore? Is this like two thousand and eight?"

"Guys calm, we're almost out." Getting silenced by Dustin, which they didn't seem to take fondly too.

This short trek was getting really tedious, and the guys were really beginning to get freaked out. Arman was getting irate with the million little questions and wanted Gary and Amir to shut up but they were unused to being followers and would bring him to his tipping point.

"Why's he in charge?" Gary only acknowledged Dustin with an arm movement, a limp flick at that.

"You mean Dustin? The guy you've known for years..." Arman's voice was getting louder and harsher sounding. "The guy who actually knows what's going on... Him?"

"Yeah!" Gary was getting ruffled. "Yeah I messed up, but we shouldn't have to leave cause his feelings got hurt... Why's he involved anyway? So I did some blow, so what." Gary's expression was one of determined steel, while Arman's became one of curious distain. Like he'd just heard the dumbest thing ever.

Dustin on the other hand couldn't hold back a loud and brash laugh, pulling them out of their asinine conversation. "Gary, just be quiet, this isn't about you."

"Then what's going on? Why are we leaving? I don't get why you don't just tell us." Gary sounded pouty, which made Arman much angrier.

Dustin simply prayed Arman would hold on for a few more moments and not loose his shit completely.

"Did I get it all?" Amir asking the group completely unphased by Gary's outburst He simply didn't want to be walking around with powder hanging from his snout.

"No, you missed some." Arman responding without taking a look.

"I'll tell you when we get a cab." Dustin was getting bored with Gary and his whining. If he wanted children he wouldn't have locked his nieces and nephews in the cellar of his families' house when he was young.

"What is the big secret?" Gary fumed. They'd exited the building finally and were moving past the door guy, a few more feet and Arman could lay into Gary all he wanted. Dustin just wished he would have a chance to calmly discuss the situation with the giant of a man who didn't appear to want any shenanigans on his watch.

"Gary shut up!" Barking, with an intense amount of anger inches away from Gary's face as he walked past. "The guy, who you got the blow from, is dead! In the men's room, probably from the same shit you guys snorted, so we're leaving!"

Arman was perhaps a tad louder than he needed to be, getting the attention of the very tall, very wide door guy Dustin wished to avoid. There was a silver lining in an instant karma type of way. It wasn't the wall of a man rising up to thunder over and interrogate Arman, presumably about drugs and the small matter of a corpse. Not that, the bright spot was, upon hearing the news he may have ingested something potentially lethal, Gary spun around hastily. Tripping over his own feet and falling hard. Luckily for him, Gary's face was spared the worst of the pavement because his hand contorted and made a loud snapping sound.

"Ow! That really hurts!" Whimpering.

About to toss Arman into the wall for those troubling words scattered across his brain like buckshot, Dustin stepped in, calmly yet definitively.

"There's a gentleman in the restroom. Last stall, he's not moving. You should go check on him." Without another word, just an exhale by Dustin, the bouncer rushed inside leaving the guys alone as if they were never there. *That was close* he thought. A second longer and the bouncer would have squished Arman and Amir into the brick to get answers. It wouldn't have been anything personal against Amir or Arman he believed, just that the bouncer didn't seem like the type to take chances. So, some mangling of the out of towner's seemed appropriate for the situation.

Confused and amazed, Arman and Amir glared at Dustin. Gary, bellowing below on the pavement was left to get up on his own. "Mind the step." Dustin ever so calm, blinked, stepped over, looking down at muscle man in some intense pain. Amir and Arman casually stepped over him as well and waited for him to get up on his own.

Gary whined the entire cab ride to the nearest hospital.

VI

Gary injured his wrist, fractured or perhaps even broken, so the end of their first night in St. Louis was spent in the emergency room waiting area. It was only half past midnight, but the boring aesthetic of white walls and depressing people mulling around, made it feel so much later. If Gary's wrist was only sprained, which was doubtful due to the loud snap they all heard and the continuing swelling that was happening around the injury, the night would have been a complete waste. Dustin didn't like seeing Gary in pain anymore than Arman did, but for a completely different reason.

Dustin didn't like seeing his snotty teary eyed inability to deal with the unfortunate curve balls life sometimes throws. To him, Gary was a ball of blubbering annoyance that should have been stuffed in a storage closet and forgotten about, but his whining brought out Arman's need to take care of other people, something almost as insufferable. But it was Arman, a true friend so Dustin staved off any ideas of shoving them in a sack and dropping them over a bridge.

Arman sat with Gary, who high as a kite and terrified his heart would explode, was in tears, believing he would die somehow. He spent the better part of the next hour begging for forgiveness. Pleading with Arman that he was worth the bother, and not to break up with him. It was getting to be a bit much. Arman soothed Gary as best he could, but in truth, Gary was starting to smell, and all the slobber was gross, so for no other reason than to be away from him, Arman tried to distract Gary by having him focus on the television set on the wall. The moving pictures and bright colors on the screen helped, some.

Amir loved watching Gary beg and squirm, but as his own high got more intense, he began blankly staring at the TV, lost in the flashing lights. Occasionally Gary and Amir's bodies would touch, and they'd get swept up in the tactile feel of each other, then Gary would go and try to use his wrist, and then cringe from pain. Arman would separate them and they'd start the whole thing over again.

It became quickly obvious what they each consumed wasn't just speed. More likely a mix of uppers and downers with something akin to molly in the mix. Mentally, Dustin pictured a bunch of pills crushed up and cut with drain opener, but it probably wasn't even that pure. Arman for some odd reason honestly thought better of Gary at one point in their relationship, sadly now, he wasn't remotely surprised that he would ingest some chemical soup without a thought as to what it was or who it was from. Gary, like the stuff the kid in the men's room overdosed on, was toxic and suffocating.

Watching Arman come to terms with this reality was brain death for Dustin, he needed to stay awake. They were in a hospital, all sorts of interesting things went on throughout the building, and they had an entire morgue that arguably was the most happening place here. Either that or the intensive care unit, it was a toss-up. He had a friend here, and if he was lucky he might see him again soon.

"I need coffee." Standing and stretching; time to wander.

"Hey Dustin, that thing with your voice. It's familiar somehow. Don't your parents use that trick?" He'd had time to process some of the weirdness. Not the dead body, that would take longer. But this, the commanding voice. He'd heard it before.

"Yeah, that's how I learned. It's why we've never been able to lie to Nate and Marta." At this point, Arman was family, time for him to see behind the curtain.

"So, can you do it back to your mom?"

"No," laughing derisively "so I've been dodging her calls. She'd open me up like a Thanksgiving turkey. It's really not fair." Shrugging.

"That only explains if she knew you were hiding something. Your mom's always been two steps ahead of us, on everything!" Arman shoved Gary off onto Amir. He was intrigued by something else now.

"That's a whole other trick. I'll explain that one later, I need to get coffee to stay awake. These two are so boring." Looking down at the Gary and Amir.

"Yeah, before you do though. In the men's room, you were talking to somebody. It was just us in there. Well, and the dead guy." Arman intended it as a question, however, with so many thoughts swirling, he just wanted to hear it out loud. "Were you doing one of those 'I see dead people' things?" Making the air quotes as if any of this made any sense.

"No, I wasn't talking to the corpse. And, I don't see dead people... Not all the time, only some of the time. Usually when I have the spare time, and when they die." Becoming a little squirrelly. "That would be silly. Like seeing everyone ever born, then all throughout their lives. That'd just be weird." Dustin made a face of 'how odd', and 'kind of gross' in its way. "Who's got the time to spy on people like that? Not me, that's for sure." A tad embarrassed and dodgy.

Arman had a thousand new questions but considering he didn't expect the response he'd gotten, "Hmm?" was about all he could get out. It was almost like Dustin wasn't being completely forthcoming so Arman sat there mouth open trying to form thoughts, and wasn't having much luck.

After a few awkward moments... "Do you want me to get you anything? Coffee, snack?" Shaking his head slowly to elicit a response.

"No, I'm okay for now. Don't get lost. They're going to see him soon, I'm guessing... And Dustin, we'll need to talk more, about, you know, everything." Such a confused look on Arman's pretty face.

"We will, it's all okay." Smiling, Dustin walked away following some corridor at the end of the waiting area. Not certain if he was going in the correct direction, he'd let the fates steer for a while. He wanted out of the conversation so he focused more on how much fun he could have in a hospital at night.

Wandering the halls for a bit, Dustin watched here and there as the hospital staff went about their duties like he was invisible. Eventually meandering into the NICU, he found himself standing at the observation window for a room full of premature babies and newborns. Some so fresh they'd just popped out of mom's oven. Nurses checking on this one and that, noticing Dustin just standing and smiling. He was harmless so they assumed he was a new parent worried over the condition of his little bundle of joy.

Like a cold shiver, a familiar fog rolled up next to Dustin, the soft fine hairs on his arm rising to connect the electric bumps with the figure intangible but present. If they could only see and feel what he did, the nursing staff may have become unnerved, even if there was no current crisis. The shade, seen only out of the corner of his hazel eyes, Dustin knew immediately who was stalking him, and no matter how he tried, he couldn't help but grin.

"They are so new and full of life." The sultry depth spoke.

"They are, how many are you calling home?" Folding his arms around himself. Dustin wasn't afraid, just unable to embrace shadows.

"Three will be returned by the next sunset. My other selves will take them. I came to check on you." Playful tones in those heady words.

"Really, you've been busy checking on me lately." Smirking wider.

"I wanted to ask you to accompany me on a task." The shadow brushing Dustin's shoulder.

It was a shock of pleasure down the spine, he'd have to hold back from expelling a groan. Wrong place for that. Dustin could only nod, turning to follow the smoke down the hall.

Shaking off the titillation so he could speak. "It seems a waste, so many new lives get sent away so soon."

"Most will be reborn in other lives quickly. Now that the human population has expanded so much, there is little waste." The smoke forming into a shape next to Dustin as they strolled the halls.

"Still, what I have trouble with is how sad it is for the parents." Ruminating on the situation. "They get so attached and don't, can't believe; it will happen to their child." Exhaling with sympathy.

"The species, in the developed world anyway, mistakenly believes every child will be born healthy, it's the illusion of the modern era."

"Very profound, I'm impressed." Almost chuckling.

"Why would you say that, I can be very profound when I want to be." If any could see the expression of this figure, they'd see it was faining at being extremely insulted.

"Please, you're usually so quiet and subdued. Also, everyone knows you're a workaholic." Dustin would have patted the person on the back if his back was a physical thing.

"Well, we're here, and after I take this dear child home, how about I take the remainder of the night off. How does that sound?" The shady shroud becoming more solid in appearance. It was time to work.

"Like a terrible idea. We both know that would be disastrous. How about part of you slips away to visit later at the hotel?" Looking upon the gauze-covered shroud, smiling with wonder, maybe even love.

"I could be persuaded perhaps, for some form of visit."

"Okay, I'd say I'll hold you too that, except well..." Gesturing, Dustin waved his hands through the mist that was a figure in front.

They'd moseyed to the pediatric care ward. Just outside the room of a young child surrounded by a mass of people. Probably loved ones, along with nurses and caregivers. Dustin quieted, putting his arms down. This was a solemn moment to be respected, the family most certainly wouldn't want a stranger intruding. "Why am I here?" whispering to the phantom.

"The child will be leaving this realm in a few ticks, she is afraid. Afraid to go, not for herself, but for her parents Julian and Ramona. I thought you might help comfort young Addi for the transition." The figure looming tall, using its form to shield Dustin's presence from the people coming and going.

"Absolutely. But they'll see me here, it may not go over well, talking to her like that." Dustin knew how confusing it was to an observer when he spoke to dead things. In this situation, it would be considered disrespectful or borderline offensive at the very least.

"If you allow me, I'll escort you across the veil, so that you may speak with her unheard and unseen by the living."

He was about to go into a lengthy explanation of how it would only be temporary, and there was nothing to fear. But then he remembered who he was talking to and skipped the orientation.

"Okay."

Because it was that easy, the shadow rolled the foggy shroud of death over Dustin sweeping him into a new reality. His vision shifted into a kaleidoscope of shapes and colors forming as the lenses focused. The gauzy shroud of grey-black mist solidified into a lanky form. Gangly like a skeleton, the flesh as it was, had a deep shade of blue-grey slate, the thin ovoid face, with dark black eyes in a cloaked hood, and mouth covered by fabric. *So, kissing him is out of the question?* The first thought that flashed across Dustin's brain. They were here to work, so perhaps afterward he'd worry about that.

"I will go and fetch the precious thing, I'll be right back." Lingering for a second too long. Dustin had to cover his smile, *death was a huge dork*, he almost belched out, remembering they were there to work, he managed to stay quiet.

Dustin's eyes misted up as he watched the way this creature slowly waded through the room, taking care to console each and every person close to this young child. Only eight or nine, her spirit form looked so bright and strong, even as her physical form reflected the opposite. A warm touch on the back or neck as the spirit of death passed the parents, a sign of respect for their loss, and an acknowledgement he had come to escort their daughter on.

With each caress the person touched knew in their heart the child had passed on, tears began flowing from the parents, holding tighter to

Addi's hands. Addi opened her eyes, her form anew and refreshed as death reached down to help her out of her body. The deceased frame of a sickly corpse lay in the middle of the bulky hospital bed. The beeps and buzzing machinery slowed as the chimes from the life support subsided. The tubes and hoses connecting the hollow frame to the world of the waking, now meaningless. As Addi rose, resplendent in death, her soul reflected what her body could not.

A full head of black hair, tussling down her back, the party dress she wished she could have worn at her birthday manifesting. Giving her aura form. Addi Ramirez-Fuller, as it read on her body's wrist tag, now in her spiritual form, healthy and radiant. So full of energy and power in the arms of the shade, as it walked back to Dustin out in the hallway. The girl's big full eyes staring at her parents now further and further from her grasp.

"I want to stay with them." Almost bellowing, pleading to the figure bringing her on.

"I'm sorry Addi, it's not their time." Death tried to sound sympathetic, but she wasn't having it.

"No! I don't want to go, I want to stay with my mom and dad." No tears, but a face full of stubborn defiance.

"Hi. Addi is it? I'm Dustin." Waving with a broad grin. It was enough to get her attention.

"Are you dead too?" Eyeing the man up and down suspiciously. Like all recently deceased, she could tell something was off about this scene.

"No, but I was invited to see you off." Attempting to convey some sort of authority. Dustin fumbled at it badly.

"Why?"

"Well, because my friend thought you were feisty. He was right, you are. Worried about your parents?"

Addi had to think on his words a moment. "What's feisty?"

"It just means you're full of pluck, you're strong and tough. It's a good thing." It had been a while since Dustin spoke with kids, he was rusty on the lingo.

"You're weird." She made a pinchy face at him, but just for a second. "My parents will be sad without me."

"Yeah, for a little bit. But they'll see you again, and you'll know they'll be okay." Dustin could feel the energy radiating off this kid. She was like a miniature sun.

"You don't know." Looking down from death's arms to this small man. Addi's arm, cradled around the head of death, his arms holding her weight, well, if she had any. In this dimension, she may have mass, or not. That was a discussion for another time, in another reality.

"He does. Dustin is wiser than most know. That's why I asked him to be here with us." The tones in the phantom's voice gave off a certain charm, all sweet and flowery when he spoke about Dustin. *Someone had a crush!*

"You're funny." Addi looked death in its big black eyes, her light reflecting back at her.

"Thank you. I think?" Not usually at a loss for words, but then again, death wasn't known for showing off to impress a guy he was into.

"Addi, he is funny, and he means well. You know that; you can feel it; right?" She nodded, her attention back on Dustin. "You can also feel what will happen with your parents, can't you?"

"I think, I'm not sure." Her face was getting scrunchy, she was trying to perceive something beyond her years and it was hard for her to express.

"It's okay. Are you worried about your parents forgetting you?" Start with the basics and go from there.

"No, but I was so weak and funny looking, they'll be sad about that." Her cheeks were getting flush. The dear spirit was self-conscious.

"I was about your age when my granny Lucy passed on, she had the same thought. Felt she was old and ugly, all wrinkled up. She reached out after she left her body and felt the memories of all of us present. That's not what the living remember." Smiling at the girl, smiling for his grandmother. Dustin's memories reaching out to this spirit and others wandering the corridors.

Their presence attracted other ghosts. Apparitions really. Psychic impressions of all the life and death that passed through this hospital. Like faded memories, they held on to the material plane. The attachments to the souls of things long gone, able to take solace in Dustin's memories.

"I see her." Making a meek smile. Addi saw a mental flash of Dustin's memory.

"Yeah, and you can see what your parents remember. It's not the dark circles under the eyes, the boney body, or the bald head." Addi gave Dustin a rather snotty look for that.

"Humph!"

He shook his head and continued. "It's their beautiful little girl, with her full head of hair. A bright smile, and the kindness in her heart. You know they will always see you for how strong and brave you are. And how many more people will know, from the strength you give them." Smiling at the now content child.

"Okay." Addi tried not to be too happy, but the more she opened to the feelings of love felt for her, it was hard to resist.

"I told you he was wise. Now, young lady, we must journey on, there are some people who would like to meet you." The soft kindness in death's voice reassured her and made Dustin a tad jealous.

"Is he coming with us?"

"No, it's not Dustin's time. He has to stay in the land of the living for now." Boo, he wasn't invited along. Death nodded to Dustin, the longing to be with him clear in his wrappings, making ready to depart.

"Before you guys go, do either of you know where I can get a cup of coffee. I've been wandering around for hours, and can't find the cafeteria." This was just a lame ploy, an attempt to be aloof to deaths seduction. The rosy cheeks gave away the ruse.

"The nurses always went that way for coffee for mom and dad." Addi pointed down the hall behind Dustin. Then she and the shadow departed as he returned to the other side of the veil.

Around twenty minutes later a refreshed Dustin waltzed into Gary's room, smiling like a man with a secret. Coffee in hand, he watched while Amir sat bored at the end of the bed watching the television mindlessly. Arman fussed with Gary's tourniquet, Gary high as a kite, fidgeting in place.

"How is he?" taking a sip. The nurse's station had surprisingly good coffee. *Who knew*?

"Where have you been? You've been gone for hours!" Arman worried, glared at Dustin.

The glaring, was because he had to watch the children by himself, and the coffee he got was the swill dispensed for visitors in tiny foam cups. Dustin had a full twenty-four once paper cup, and it smelled so aromatic. The smell of the flavorful odor over the host of antiseptic, and other less wondrous hospital aromas lingering in the room. So for that, it was good, and Arman squinted at his friend, he was super envious.

"It's hard to find a good cup of coffee in this place. Sorry." He wasn't.

"It's fine, dumbass broke his wrist. Were waiting for him to be discharged." Giving up on the sling, and Gary.

"What about?" referring to the dazed Iranian, blankly watching infomercials, and fidgeting gym bunny, who were no doubt at differing places in their trip.

"I don't know how, and I didn't ask, but the doctor didn't say anything about them being fucked up. Gary held it together, somehow." Arman looked like he really wanted to smother Gary with a pillow.

"We gotta go, I can't sit still." In hushed tones, Gary's eyes were wide, almost fully dilated. Yet strangely he didn't try to get up, sitting perfectly still, merely twitching his arms.

"Tonight was a bust, I need a drink." Giving up on the lukewarm mud, Arman set the hospital coffee on the counter by the sink.

"We did get that upgraded room, with all sorts of booze in it." Dustin was so chipper, it begged more questions, but that would be for later.

"What do you think we should do with these idiots?" Arman sighed.

"We could dump their asses in Amir's room. Who knows, maybe they'll wake up in a compromising position." Grinning at the thought of that.

"That would be too good to be true, imagine them doing it, we'd need pictures." Surveying the frenemies, what a lark.

"Well they'd try, but I bet they've both got tina-dick."

"Eww." The thought flipped Arman's stomach.

"How about we drop them off, grab some bottles, and head down to the pool to drink ourselves silly...?"

The thought of their two limped dick friends making attempts at sloppy sex wasn't going to deter Dustin. The night was still young. Somewhere, it was pushing two in the morning as they gathered up everybody's stuff.

"Think it'll be open? At this hour." Sketchy, but not a lot of options.

"No, but who cares, we're leaving tomorrow anyway." That settled it.

VII

Unable to get through to Jordon, Arman and Dustin piled their strung-out friends into the back of a cab. Raced away from the hospital, making one quick stop at an all-night convenience store for snacks and two liters, then straight back to the hotel. The city at night was eerily quiet, at least as far as a normal person would notice. Dustin being rather odd in his way got to view the city through a different lens. All sorts of multicolored pops and fizzes, noises from those things that go bump in the night. The strangeness that cause normal folks to look over their shoulders when they walk an empty street.

From his perspective, the city was hopping. It was the jolt of excitement he needed to wake up and commit minor violations of the criminal code. Marching the two men up to the single room, Dustin and Arman ditched them on the bed, grabbed a couple of bottles of booze, and prepared to sneak into the gated pool after hours.

Like good hoodlum's, the two filled up one of Dustin's knapsacks with snacks, cups, booze, and mixers while Arman was in charge of towels and changes of shorts tucked into his jaunty over the shoulder bag. They didn't feel the need to lug a bunch of junk around just in case they'd have to hop a fence or sneak about. Knowing there was an ice machine on the way, they'd use that as their cover to skulk past any security; Mission Impossible style. A slick scheme to park their asses in some secluded corner of the pool area to drink themselves into a stupor.

I was very thrilling slinking about, like when they were high school, and wholly unneeded. Dustin and Arman weren't the first to sneak into the pool. In fact, there seemed to be an after-hours party for some of the staff and friends. By all accounts, one of the lifeguards was entertaining friends and strangers alike in a makeshift pool house. The older white building housing the equipment turned into a party den. Music and muffled noise emanating from the dimly lit structure.

After six or so offers to join them in the "party" by several visibly erect men coming and going; they were certain they wouldn't get ratted out for hanging on the far end, tucked into the plastic lounge chairs.

"They'll be okay up in the room right?" Arman asked, only after he and Dustin got situated and a bit tipsy.

"They should be."

"But you'll like, be able to know if something's wrong? Right?" His bright brown eyes imploring Dustin.

"No. Look, I'm sure they'll be fine. The odds are they're going to tire themselves out eventually." Dustin spoke matter of factly, spoiling any sense of awe and wonder for Arman.

"Why not?"

"What do you mean why not? I'm not psychic, I can't foresee danger. Look, if they die, I might be able to sense that... Or not."

"A lot of weird things happened today, centered around you. So how does it work? Come on mister wizard, spill."

"Look, sometimes I see when a spirit passes into death, or is born. The inbetween part; that's someone's life. It's not an all the time thing and I don't really have much say over how or when it comes on." Lying to Arman and to himself some. Dustin never explored the extent of his abilities; it was simply an aspect of his person, like peeing. It happened when it needed to.

"That's no fun. You said you'd explain. The voice thing, how your parents know stuff before we do it? What about you? What can you do? Come on Dustin, t-e-l-l m-e!" Arman begged like a small puppy wanting attention.

"That's a trick passed down on my mom's side of the family. From my grandmothers to my mother. She hasn't taught me everything yet. According to grandma Hester, granny Lucy taught Marta how to do all that when mom was little. It has something to do with projecting her spirit to the astral plane where the curvature of time is more apparent."

Dustin was speaking inbetween slugging back a rather large cocktail. He was so accustomed to this, it was somewhat boring talking about. "Grandma Hester's a lousy teacher, and Marta is only teaching me in stages." Shrugging. "I can astral project at times, but other than that, I'm waiting for Marta to teach me what she knows."

Arman on the other hand just made a completely blank face, confused by the words uttered between gulps. "Fine, don't tell me."

"What?" Shocked Arman didn't believe him. "That's how Marta explained it to me. Mom promised to finish teaching me when I'm ready. I was like five when she promised, and I'm still waiting for her to keep that promise." Dustin used his 'in all seriousness' look.

"I'm so much more confused than I was at the bar." Getting pouty.

"The commanding. That's easy; anybody can do it with practice. It's all about keeping calm and using only words that matter. Words that take and hold attention." Dustin was doing his best to assure Arman his world view wasn't completely off its rocker.

"Harrumph! That's just a bunch of new age bull crap." Arman wasn't buying this load.

"Sorry, from my perspective, it's like applied science. You know what my families like, so it's not that far fetched. That was the normal I grew up with." Weird was so normal to Dustin, he couldn't really clarify it without examples.

They sat and drank for another twenty minutes or so. Watching as men came and went from the bunkhouse, taking a break, cooling down by doing a few laps in the pool. It was a pretty festive group coming and going from the storage unit, now playpen. And so much fun to watch all the eye candy run amok naked. Gary and Amir would be so envious if they knew this was happening. Both Dustin and Arman would make sure to tell each of them every steamy detail, just to watch their faces contort with jealousy.

The drinks settling into Arman's system, he began reminiscing about times gone by with Dustin, and how long they'd known each other. Dustin's family, parents, grandmother, assorted aunts and cousin's, all in one house. A house that had a million or so people coming and going, stopping by or departing at all hours of the night.

And most importantly, no matter what strange batshit crazy thing happened, and there always seemed to be something happening; Dustin and folks acted calm cool and collected.

Rarely could Arman remember a time when he'd approach the house and someone wouldn't be holding the door ready to direct Arman to wherever Dustin was at. Upon entry, someone, any number of the faces Arman recognized, had a kind word, gave some helpful advice, and usually offered him some snack as though he'd been expected. Dustin's family never acted caught off guard by anything.

"Dustin, do you remember when we met?" Raising his brow, Arman had a few thoughts rattling around his brain by the look of it.

"Yeah, second grade. On the playground. And later when you showed up at my house with your mom." All nonchalant.

"Uh, yeah. I was thinking mostly about when Troy Alder wanted to smash your face in. I couldn't understand why he had such a bug up his butt?" The details for Arman were just past the tip of memory. For such a profound moment in his life, his recollection was foggy.

"He was just upset because Chad Warren overheard me talking about his dad's affair. He wasn't going to do anything about it." To Dustin, this was ancient history.

"Yeah, he was! He wanted to kill you." Arman got his serious face on.

"No, he wanted to berate me for being, what he considered was weird." Shrugging.

"You were weird, everyone knew you were weird. But how'd Chad hear you talking about it, you sat alone every day under the tree by the jungle gym?" Some pieces of Arman's strange friend started falling into place. "Until me, no kid in school spoke to you!"

"Well yeah. Didn't mean I didn't have friends."

"No, you didn't! Everyone thought you were possessed and was afraid of you." Taking a deep breath, Arman got a touch twitchy. "Everyday it was some odd thing happening around you. The lights going out in our classroom, but just around you. Or when you wanted something in the cafeteria and they only had just enough for you... Like popsicles, we never got popsicles!"

"The lights only went out when I was bored."

"So, you were always bored... Dude you freaked everybody out all the time. That's why you didn't have friends."

"Maybe not the way you think of friends, but I had a lot of friends. And I got popsicle's anytime I wanted, plus you got over it. You came over and stood up to Troy. You didn't need too, but it was appreciated." Looking sideways at Arman with a knowing gaze, Dustin understood more than he was saying.

"I have to tell you something about that." After all this time Arman wanted to clear the air on how they became friends.

"That you only stood up for me on a dare?" Dustin sat casually as ever, drinking.

"How'd you know, I never told you that?" Arman was taken aback.

"It wasn't a secret Pamela Cartwright dared you to intervene. You told Pam I was weak and would get my ass beat." Dustin stayed completely chill. "So, she dared you to be a big man and stop Troy."

"How could you possibly know that? And why the hell didn't you say anything about it? Dustin, I've felt guilty about that ever since. I should have told you." Arman was getting a bit too emotional over the old days for Dustin's liking.

"Sorry. But there was nothing to say. We became friends and you have no reason to feel guilty for anything." Shrugging. What else was there to do?

"You let me carry around that burden all these years." Arman's eyes got a little misty. He wanted some appreciation by the look of it.

"Are you upset with me? Arman, I appreciate the friendship, but I wasn't a charity case. You didn't have to step in and save the day." Frowning slightly at Arman.

"No you ass! Not for confronting Troy. My mom overheard Pam and Chad and me in the living room. She heard them teasing me about the dare. My mom thought it was cruel that I only pretended to be your friend, so she made me go over to your house." Arman folded his arms, scowling.

Dustin thought on Arman's words for a moment and when he spoke, Arman was a bit more perplexed than he thought he'd be. "Well, that's stupid."

"What the?" Arman sat up, spinning so that he was on the edge of the pool chair, feet on the pavement. Dustin was not acting like the person he thought he knew at all.

"That's why you and your mom showed up to our house? I guess it makes sense." Dustin just squinted slightly, thinking back. Arman made a face like he wanted to be mad, but the sheer confusion made him look like he was having trouble taking a dump.

"You knew I was upset when I got there! The first thing you said to me when you answered the door was 'it'll be alright' then you offered me a cookie!" Arman acted a little flabbergasted. "We didn't even ring the bell. Dustin, no one ever rings the doorbell. You guys just open it before anyone rings and offer people food! What's that about?" Emotions coming up from somewhere deep inside.

Odd should have been Dustin's middle name. It was actually Thaddeus, however, Arman had to focus on the matter at hand. Clutching his drink unable to use words for a hot second he did what most people would do and shot-gunned his cocktail.

"I thought you were being clingy. I mean we just met, and you showed up at my house a few hours later." Dustin made an *I'm sorry* scrunchy face. "If we're confessing things..."

"What, you're going to tell me you're an alien?" Sarcasm dripped from Arman's full pouting lips.

"No brat. Nate and I had a talk when I got home from school. I didn't want to be friends with you." Taking a breath.

"Why not?" That felt like a stab in the heart to Arman.

"I didn't like how mean you were. Troy was going to have a bad enough time at home when his parents divorced, and he didn't need you beating him up." Dustin had such empathy in his face.

"Oh. Wow, I hadn't even considered that. I never thought about how you'd think of the situation." He sat staring at his feet for a few minutes. "How were you able to have any sympathy for Troy, he wanted to kill you?"

"He was acting out. Troy and his sibling's life at home was pretty rough. If he needed to feel strong by bullying me, it was okay. He was never going to hit me, Troy was more afraid of me than you were." A slight smirk formed across Dustin's mouth.

"You were really scary. In fact, you still are. Why did you say it would be alright when we got to your house?" Arman was going to get some answers, in some way, somehow.

"That's actually what I was trying to confess. The other stuff was just the tip..." Making a sideways, caught with the hand in the cookie jar pensive face.

"Okay... Do I want to know?"

"It's only fair. Your mom made you be friends with me to look out for the weak. Nate made me be friends with you because he was concerned you'd be bullied for being gay. I was supposed to look out for you." Dustin let out a sigh of relief, a burden lifted. He felt better.

"Oh my god! Our parents made us become friends to watch each other's backs?" Arman slugged quickly poured another drink and without thinking too hard on it started to slug it back.

"Looks like... You may want to slow down on that."

"And your dad thought I was gay when I was seven?" He sneered at the idea of slowing down, passing out was fast becoming the best option to end this strange night.

"Nate's gaydar has always been better than anyone else's in the family. They always knew I was, so Nate wanted me to watch out for you, just in case someone started shit." Dustin was back to being deadpan.

"Huh... Weird." Arman gulped down a third of his drink in one swig. "So, you knew about the dare, about Troy's parents, about me being gay. But you didn't know about my mom punishing me by forcing me to come over to your house?"

"Yes." Dustin's eyes widened slightly.

"Explain."

"You might not believe me if I do." He was a bit apprehensive to tell Arman, it seemed far fetched.

"After tonight, I wouldn't worry so much about that. How about you explain to me how any of this is normal for you, and I'll decide if I believe it?" Blankly starring at Dustin.

"That seems fair. Basically, it was Marcus. He told Bonetosser and she told me. Marcus wasn't around when you got in trouble with your mom. He was at my house."

"Not saying I believe you... But if that's true; my dog, told your cat, and she told you?"

"Basically yes."

"They hated each other."

"No, they were more like competitors. Those two had so much free time they sparred with each other. How else would you explain how Marcus got out of the backyard every time he wanted. Bonetosser opened the gate so they could go chase squirrels and birds and stuff."

"Dude, we got in trouble for leaving the gate open! My parents never believed it wasn't us!" Arman alarmed for some reason over this news, straightened his back.

"I didn't know you when she started doing it. But when we became friends, you didn't get in trouble for it anymore, did you?"

"No. Why was that?" Suspicion rising.

"My mom had a talk with your parents."

"Okay. I'm processing all of this, so bear with me." Taking a few long minutes. Arman had to think; this was really hurting his noggin and his buzz. "So how did you know about Troy's family?"

"The neighborhood crows. They used to flock in the tree on the playground. Some of them were such gossips. Did you know Mrs. Henley and her husband were swingers? They had a year's long affair with the Mayfair's."

"Stop! You're making that up." Arman's eyes bulged, too much more and they'd pop.

"I would never. They were into kinky latex outfits, dressing like satin's cheerleaders and devil bikers; and yeah that part; I am. I know it's strange and a lot to take in. So I didn't tell you, I'm sorry."

"Thanks. I can't say I believe you. But if this is real, which I'm not saying it is, you talk to the dead, and animals?"

"Obviously not. Not all of them."

"Oh? Good to know! Care to elaborate?"

"The dead people I told you about. Animals, well I only communicate with ones that used to be people. People who came back to make up for being shitty in their other life."

"So reincarnation, that's a thing... Dustin I'm going to lay back, close my eyes and think about how to cope with this. I'm really hoping this is a dream, but if today was, in fact, real... Then I just need some time to adjust."

"I get that. Arman, no matter what happens, I'm glad our parents forced us to become friends. That: I wouldn't change for the world."

"Me too Dustin. And I have to say dream or not, being friends with you has never been boring. Plus the sheer amount of shit we got away with, I wouldn't change that for the world." Arman closed his eyes perhaps the mirage would evaporate away.

VIII

Opening his eyes as he leaned forward on the railing of the third story balcony, Dustin gazed down at the pool area. He and Arman were passed out on the plastic lounge chairs by the far corner. Able to make out the label on the bottle nearest him, Dustin knew immediately why he went to the other place. *Rum, always makes me groggy.* He stayed awake switching to rum when Arman needed to lie down. Arman had a lot dumped on him in the way of strange. Dustin felt bad snowballing him, and let the guy sleep in peace while he drank. Dustin was a touch out of sorts after their conversation, yes it was a burden lifted, though at what cost to their friendship? He'd only know when Arman woke.

A single individual was floating around in the pool, doing a lazy backstroke. He was a rather attractive mid-fifties gentleman, with a slight paunch, and some striking grey hair. The water covered his endowment, most likely spent, as the noise from the pool house was now mainly muffled moaning.

"Ah, you're awake." That smooth as ice silky voice fogged in with the vaporous form in black behind it. The spirit from the bar, and hospital. Not one of his counterparts, the feel was the same form.

"So, this isn't a dream." Dustin propped an elbow on the railing, cocking his head at the shimmering phantom coming fully into frame.

"No. You're projecting. It's been a while since I've seen you awake on this plane." A certain lurid insinuation in the spectre's tone.

"It's been ages since I can remember astral projecting. Huh? The last time I aware of it I think was Mayday." Dustin smirked at the apparition.

"It was, you were so young at the time. But now you're all grown up." Its words causing Dustin's spine to tingle.

"I was thirteen. You were there? I mean of course you were, but you, you?" Dustin focused more on the context of his speech than the ominous figure in black slowly moving in his direction.

"I know what you mean. Yes, I was visiting and stayed to watch. You were quite entertaining." It's form manifesting, almost completely solid.

"I got into so much trouble! But it was so fun. I don't remember seeing you, I looked."

"I was in the old ash tree, on the northern side of the maypole. The tree was making ready to say goodbye."

"I did see you! I thought you were the Lord of the Wild. I waved before I flew off into the stars." Dustin smiled broadly.

"That was me. The Lord of the Wild was spending time with the Mayqueen in another part of the wood." The wrapping around the grim creature's mouth moved as if he smiled.

"I wish Nate and Marta were somewhere else, the only time I was ever grounded was from that night. Just for being high."

"And climbing to the top of the maypole. Then falling off."

"There was that, but in all fairness, that's what my mom gets for leaving the flying suave out in the open." Dustin wagged his finger at the entity.

"I hope you didn't get into too much trouble. I didn't feel you for several years after that." The spirit was pensive, apprehensive even.

"Lectured mostly. About swinging around the top of the maypole, scaring everyone. Stealing my mom's drugs. You know, stupid stuff." Dustin lamenting on the days of yore. "Nate's cousin Marlow still whines about how he injured his back catching me. All the time with the guilt." Dustin shook his head. Everything comes with a price he supposed.

"Marlow Ney. Injured himself trying to impress a young maiden by carrying a keg that was much too heavy for him. He was nowhere near you when you fell." The grin beneath the gauze wrap was almost visible. The apparition seemed gleeful.

"That jackass! I've had to hear him bitch for years. He's on my list." Dustin stood to attention, pretending to be mad.

"I'm relieved that was all, I believed Hester felt I was coming for you."

"No. Grandma Hester wasn't worried about that. She and my parents decided I needed to be punished so I wouldn't mess with toxic shit without knowing what I was doing."

"Oh, what happened?" Hesitating like an overeager date who wants to get it on. "If I may ask?"

"Of course. I spent the rest of the summer at the farm. She taught me all about herblore. I missed baseball season, but who cares. It was the best summer of my life." Dustin's eyes sparkled. "After that, I just sort of kept living. Sorry I haven't been around much." Thus the difference between them, one alive one not.

"Don't apologize, you're so self-effacing. You noticed me when you were able, and life is for living. It should be enjoyed." The black pools of darkness that were this forms eyes glowed down into Dustin with something akin to love. "Plus, it's not like I wasn't going to see you again." After he said it, he felt his words might be misconstrued as awkward.

"Relax, I get it." Not able to hold back a chuckle. "So, are you here on business or pleasure?" Dustin felt his blood get flush inside this non-corporeal shell.

Even intangible Dustin was amazed at how solid the world was. A touch, a vibration; a simple thing like hearing one's own laugh was coherent and real. The world around him the same except his physical body was passed out in a drunken stupor on a pool chair.

"I could lie and say I'm going your direction, but you'd see right through me."

"Because I can. The shadow's all misty." Dustin passed his gaseous hand through the spectre's gaseous body for jest.

"So, I will simply say that I wanted to reconnect, get to know you as an adult." A smirk of sorts behind the shroud.

"I see. Tell me, did you by chance have anything to do with the rooms? You know the pipe, and that little accident the honeymoon couple suffered?" Time to get to the brass tax. Dustin had the spirit on the ropes and how he answered would decide his fate.

"I'm shocked you would think such a thing. I would never use my position to alter the course of natural events to an outcome." The flamboyant hand over heart gesture only worked for people who had hearts. Even then, not all that often.

"Um, hum."

"I did nothing I would not have normally done. That being said, I merely moved the bacteria in the pipe to where a leak would happen. They still would have died. However, the leak would just have taken place while you were in the room." The shadowy figure's tone tried to sound heroic.

"Well thank you, that was very kind of you." Dustin made an exaggerated gentile bow. "What about the couple?" His tone became much firmer.

"Oh that. Well, I simply presented them with a choice. It was purely by happenstance. A bird was hit by a vehicle just moments before they drove by. I only revealed myself while I worked. They decided to careen off the road. It was their decision." His tone became a little bit snotty.

Dustin broke into a laugh. For the second time to an outside observer, he was mocking this couple's tragedy. He'd have to send a card or something.

"I have to admit, you make a damn good impression when you want to reconnect with someone." Leaning in, this was it. Dustin was going to kiss this big smoggy fool on its gauze covered mouth area.

The shadow could best be described as blushing, however, without a visible face, it was a moot point. And as he leaned in to receive a kiss he's waited for, his attention was drawn down to the pool. The shroud turned leaving Dustin close to planting a smooch on the side of the spectre's face area. That would have been a buzz kill, luckily his attention was likewise pulled to the pool area.

Dustin's dear friend Arman was in panic mode, pulling and tugging at Dustin's body to respond. It wasn't the body in the chair he was concerned about, but the sinking form of the man in the pool.

"I should collect him while I'm here." The phantom made it sound like work or something.

"Did he drown?"

"No, a blood vessel in his brain burst. He felt only a twinge of pain."

"That's good at least, I guess I have to wake up as well." Equally flat.

"Dustin, oh my god, he needs help!" Arman shouted as Dustin rose up, opening his eyes.

Without any further hesitation, Arman dove into the pool and snatched the body up, hopefully before it drowned. He couldn't know it was too late. Dustin knew because his make-out session got interrupted before it started.

In the water, splashing around, Arman shouted. "Help, someone help!" Pulling at the once handsome daddy. "Dustin, help me get him out of the water!" Demanding.

Dustin stood up, felt his head swoon and slowly plodded to the edge to help lift the lifeless body out of the water.

Hearing a screaming queen in the dead of night at a sex party tends to get attention, so a few heads turned. The shrieks and screams from Arman attempting to be helpful brought some folks out of the makeshift bungalow. Rushing to their aide, several party goer's, two of which actually had their junk covered, helped Arman and Dustin lift and pull the man from the pool.

Dustin stood up and pulled a bewildered Arman back so the man's friends could attempt to resuscitate him. As more people flowed out of the pool house the crowd was growing and the scene would soon be mobbed. Dustin began gathering up their things as the shadow reformed, the daddy in tow.

"He was hung." Dustin noted. It was lost on Arman, but not the spirit.

"If you like that sort of thing." Sounding pissy.

"Oh, sugar, he's got nothing on you." Dustin was quite pleased he could see the form of the shade as well as the ghost of the mortal as if they were standing there in the flesh. A connection was definitely building.

Arman glared at Dustin, again talking to someone he couldn't see. And again acting aloof to the fact there was a dead body not more than a few feet away from him.

"Are you insane? A guy's dying and you're flirting with what? Air?" Arman was beginning to shake, not because he was mad, or cold and wet, but probably due to shock.

"No." Dustin remained calm as he looked from the spirit to Arman and back. "Is there a way he can see?" Asking the shadow.

"Take his hand, if you trust him, then he may."

Dustin, without waiting for Arman to trip over his next words took his hand, holding it firmly.

With the sudden appearance of a naked body that was also lying on the pavement ten feet away, and the shadowy phantom wrapped and mummified in black, Arman tried to flee. Yet for some reason he couldn't. Perhaps it was some supernatural strength on Dustin's part who held firm to Arman's hand. Or perhaps, it was Arman, weak in the knees and sick to his stomach from the shock of it all.

"What in the name of the almighty god is this shit?" He bellowed.

Some of the people close to the guy on the ground glowered at Arman, but seeing as he was all wet and shaking, chalked it up rightfully to shock. He was with someone so they let him be.

"Arman it's alright. The shadow isn't here to hurt anyone. He's just escorting this man home." Lowering his voice so as Arman would be the only one to hear what would be considered insane ramblings of a deranged man.

The frightened corpse mouthed his name, a notion he didn't want to go off into the void without being remembered. Pushing towards his lifeless body, the shadow held him gently back. There was no returning to his empty life, or an emptier shell. Like the girl in the hospital; Addi, Dustin reached out and found his memories. He was worried for no good reason.

"His name is Jason Grant. When he and his boyfriend broke up, he took it pretty hard. He's afraid he died without ever being loved." Dustin's voice using the commanding tone, combined with the look of intent compassion settled Arman just enough so that he could take in what was happening.

"How do you know that?" Arman watched the corpse's expression of sadness and pain and somehow understood Dustin was right.

"Jason told me." Looking past the ghost into the blackness, Dustin saw something else. "Jason. You are loved, someone's waiting for you on the other side. He waited all this time for you to join him. Follow the ferryman, he'll take you to Mitchell." Dustin's eyes sparkling again. The dead guys face brightened. For a ghost, it had a new reason to go on.

"I best get this gentleman on his way then. He has a long journey." The shadow split in two. One form moving with the body away, dissolving into nothingness. The other standing, looking like a wanting puppy. "It had to be the ferryman. That will take some of me ages. You know how he likes to prattle on. I swear he needs to get out more." Acting a bit pouty before slowly evaporating.

"Sorry. But you're the one who showed me." Smirking. Dustin loved this, but Arman acted as if he was about to vomit and piss himself. All color was rushing from his face, he was beginning to look down right caucasian, like out of Omega Man. Not a pretty look as far as Dustin was concerned.

"Will I at least get to see you later?" Asking as his cloaked head faded ever so slowly.

"I hope so." *Wanton hussy.* Dustin mused.

Departed with the departed, the shadow faded completely as Dustin released Arman and finished gathering up their things. "I'm hallucinating!" Arman felt his brain flooded with weirdness and booze.

"You're not hallucinating. Let's get our stuff and go." Dustin grabbed the bottles and tucked the last of their things into the bags.

"I'm not going anywhere!" Arman in shock reacted in a rather snotty voice. "I feel like I'm tripping my balls off."

"Okay, then at least have a seat and take a towel to dry off." Pulling a towel out from Arman's bag, Dustin passed it to him and sat on the edge of the lounge chair.

Arman accepted the towel, pulling it around him while pacing for a minute or so until the nausea subsided. Eventually sitting as more people flooded out to the pool. The two sat quietly for a little bit as the crowd grew and questions began flying around. Soon the lights from squad cars could be seen and about twenty minutes after the death of the man in the pool, the cops arrived with the paramedics. Shortly thereafter Brad, the guy from the front desk arrived on scene, visibly upset and shaken by a death at the hotel.

Once he was able to speak, Arman asked: "Why did you want to leave?"

"It's all the questions. They bug me. How'd it happen, why? Was there anything anyone could do, this that and the other." Dustin got a rather angry glare from Arman. "Folks act like death is so ominous and scary. People pass on when they pass on, and often I know how and why, but to say anything? People don't believe me, so I usually avoid the questions." The glare softened.

"But do you know? How do you really know the guy's name or anything about him?" Arman wanted Dustin to be wrong. He was trying to disprove something he suspected was true.

"I just do. Listen for yourself, ask them. Someone in this crowd knows who he is." Dustin had the outward appearance of calmness, however underneath there was some apprehension. He was more concerned if Arman thought him to be a liar than anything else.

Arman listened, heard Brad talk with the cops. The man's name was dropped here and there. Arman would want to confirm, but it was out there. The cops talked to some other people and then they turned their attention to the lounge chairs. More appropriately to Arman and Dustin sitting quietly on the lounge chairs. An officer walked over to the still wet Arman and asked the obligatory questions.

"Do you know what happened?" Very nice and polite in a contempt-filled manner.

"I woke up from a nap hearing a sound, saw the guy jolt and go under." Arman recalling the events. His voice was shaky, Arman was still a bit rattled. This sort of thing didn't happen to him often.

"And you?" the average looking police officer was very nondescript. *Such a stereotype* Dustin thought. His voice and face had the same matching trait... Bland.

"Arman woke me, and he dove in to pull the guy out. He shouted and some guys came running to help and we pulled him out of the pool." Dustin's voice was flat and methodical. Almost as if the officer would get drowsy if he kept listening.

"Did either of you know him, or were with him this evening?" The undercurrent of disgust was apparent in the officer's voice. Hinting that Dustin and Arman may have been two more men involved in some wild sex party that got out of control.

"No. We were out here, off to the side all night. We had a long drive and just wanted some quiet time outside, alone." The methodical words spooling from Dustin's mouth sent the local cop into a slight trance.

Dustin spoke volumes with few words. They were to be left in peace and were nowhere near anyone or anything. As far as this officer was concerned, they didn't exist. He simply turned, walked back to the other police on the scene and could be heard saying "They didn't know anything." And that was it as far as the cops were concerned.

"You made him leave didn't you?" Whispering.

"He was being a dick." Dustin sneered at the cop.

An agitated Brad made his way over to Arman and a lesser extent, Dustin. Most of the people Brad spoke to, couldn't remember if Dustin helped or not. Brad was much more civil than the officer when he stopped by.

"Mr. Salad -naively... Uh, sorry." Brad blushed, attempting and tripping terribly over the name.

"Salah-Navuluri. You can call me Arman."

"Thank you. I wanted to thank you for attempting to rescue him." Brad wasn't sure if he should try to shake Arman's hand or not. Arman hadn't stopped clutching his towel.

"Dustin helped me pull him out of the water."

"Oh." A bit surprised for some reason. "Well thank you both. You gentlemen didn't happen to be apart of the..." Brad gestured to the pool house and the insinuation that it entailed.

"Ew! No." In unison, they squealed.

"That's good. I'm sorry this happened, apparently, some of the staff have been using the facilities after hours for personal reasons; so to speak." Brad was trying to find something to do with his hands, he seemed jittery.

"Does anyone know him? The guy from the pool." Arman asked tentatively.

"Oh, yes. He checked in yesterday. Such a nice man." The sadness on Brad's face didn't look genuine. More like he was sad at not being able to score with such a hot daddy, rather than the drowning.

Arman figured why not ask? "What was his name?" He wanted the confirmation.

"I shouldn't. It's policy to respect our guest's privacy."

"Oh, it's just us, you can spill." Dustin giving him a push.

"Jason Grant. He was so sexy, I flirted with him so hard when he came in. But he was upset because he just ended things with someone."

Lusty blushing taking hold of Brad's face. "Great job, great bod, and by the looks of it, a great dick... Why would anyone break up with him, I mean really?" Brad began to ramble on. "I was going to ask him to dinner tomorrow. I guess it's too late." He lamented for a tad too long.

"Sorry to hear that. Say, Brad... Due to some of the events of the night, we haven't been able to get much sleep. Is there any way we could push back our checkout time?" Not fazed by corpses or hormonal males pondering what ifs, Dustin figured someone had to watch out for their merry band of idiots.

"I suppose so, what, if I may ask; happened to your friends?" Polite, and of course he'd acquiesce, however, the back of Brad's brain spooled with thoughts about the other guys who showed up with these two.

"They're upstairs acting like? Well; you met them, so you know."

Arman didn't need to use any kind of commanding voice, it was Gary he was talking about. The mention of the others gave him the anger to show it in his face and voice. Brad who could empathize easily, nodded his head.

"Absolutely, after tonight, I think I'll have no trouble finding rooms. Would five be too early?"

Trying to move pieces around in his head. Brad's face contorted at the thought of loosing business due to the untimely death of a sexy guest. That sort of thing often put a damper on the vacation plans of shallow look obsessed men who would do it with anything that moved. By his body language and posture Brad wanted to be one of those things that moved.

"No. That's more than generous. It'll give us time to eat and get on the road before sundown. Thank you." The charm in Dustin's voice, so out of character and glittery, tickled Brad's spine.

Brad nodded and left them feeling great about meeting Arman and *that wonderful man Dustin.* For some reason, he couldn't for the life of him understand how he could have ever forgotten that guy. *The one he just had a good feeling about?* The one who now, a second later he couldn't picture. *Like he didn't exist.* Brad had no idea what he was thinking about just moments before. *However, those guys in the lover's suite could stay as long as they wanted.*

Dustin didn't feel bad messing with Brad mind. Brad was needy as far as Dustin was concerned and would feel compelled to get all up in their business if he wasn't checked. Dustin really didn't want him hovering around talking about his fantasies with the guests. He probably overreacted, but in his defense, Dustin only cared about Arman's feelings and was worried he might think of Dustin as a freak. Thus tearing a hole in their friendship.

"You messed with his mind didn't you?" Arman squinted narrowly at Dustin.

"A little bit."

"Don't do that to me." Arman's face flat and stern looking.

"Only if you stop freaking out about the dead."

"I can't promise that. It's not every day I see a walking corpse!"

"They can't hurt you and they're not corpses. They're just people who aren't alive anymore. Kind of spirit like in a way." Dustin tried to keep a straight face. Arman was reacting much better than he believed he would.

"That means they're dead. And who was the thing you were flirting with?" His attention shifting quickly, Arman had a new set of questions.

"It wasn't like that." A minute amount of red in Dustin's cheeks appeared.

"Uh-hmm. 'Will I see you later, I hope so'..." Mocking Dustin and the shroud covered person. "Who was that?"

"That was, is, in a nutshell; a personification of the masculine principle for the moment when life ends." More red and a slight smirk. Dustin wasn't as calm as he always came across.

"When life ends: Is death. You were flirting with death!" Arman was both appalled and titillated. This made a certain sense. Dustin's taste in guys had always been a bit spooky.

"Yes in a way, he's more like the Roman god Viduus. He pulls the souls from bodies. But he's not really a god, more of an underlying universal force." Dustin began rambling, blushing more and more.

"Oh my god, your totally geeking out. You do like him! You always go geek, when you like a guy, you're such a freak!" Arman began chuckling, he needed to see Dustin lose his calm to deal with the strange.

"What? I'm just trying to get him to ask me out. It's no big. I want to see if there's anything there." Averting his gaze to hide how flustered he was getting.

"You're trying to get a date with death, and it's no big?" Arman stood, this was a new kind of strange altogether. "You're so weird." Grabbing up his bag.

"He's a great guy. I've known him my entire life... And frankly, most of the guys I meet are boring compared to him." Dustin clutched his bag, this was getting too personal for the pool crowd still amassed.

"Oh my god, Dustin. You've known the grim reaper your whole life and want to what? Date him?" Arman for some reason was pleased as punch by these revelations, although his brain should say to be terrified. Such an odd mix.

"Can we talk about this up in the room?" Dustin used hushed tones. Too many hungry ears wanting a scoop.

"You're beet red! The always calm and collected Dustin Ney is blushing. Wait until I tell the guys." Arman followed Dustin as he made a quick exit into the hotel.

"I am not."

"You so are. I've never seen this side of you. It's cute. So tell me, how have you known mister spooky your whole life?" More questions, now intriguing and fun questions to annoy and fluster an unflappable Dustin with.

"He's a friend of the family." Head down in fully flushed red.

"No wonder you didn't have friends growing up, death is part of the family!" Arman couldn't believe it, but now Dustin's odd home life made so much more sense. The voice, the dead people, death. "You're the fricking Adams Family!".

"We are not!" Sounding shrill. "I had lots of friends. Just that, not all of them were; human."

"I'll bet, hiding any monsters in that house of yours?"

"Just your boyfriend!" Arman smacked Dustin in the back for that comment. "Ow!"

"Ex-boyfriend, I'm dumping him!"

"At least do it at dinner, after today we need some comic relief." With that, they were at the door to the suite. Both chuckling and most importantly, their friendship intact.

IX

Tired and beleaguered from the long night and the many questions, Dustin grabbed his overnight bag and slumped on the bed. Arman was very glad the unusual events subsided, or at least he believed they did. Dustin had a lingering thought a friend might show up once they got settled in.

After a spell, mostly due to Arman being soaked to the bone, a bit rattled and shaken into sobriety it was decided he would check on the cuddle puddle in the adjoining room to make sure they were finally asleep. Or at the very least not freaking out too badly. While he was away Dustin changed into his bedclothes, a ratty old pair of jammies he'd kept for years, comfort clothes. They were an old set of black pajamas with red and white sugar skulls across them. He received them as a gift from Arman when they went off to college.

Appeased the guys in the next room were behaving Arman returned making himself a late night drink. "They're twitching and naked, but it looks like they're asleep." His expression looked so much more relieved knowing he wouldn't have to babysit.

"Sometimes you just have to let the children tucker themselves out." Dustin smirked.

"Thanks dick."

"You were the one who wanted kids."

"Yeah, yeah, yeah. You're ready for bed already? Sure you don't want to prowl around the graveyard to find your lover's corpse?" Arman sneered.

"He's not a corpse, and I don't need to prowl." With that, Dustin pointed behind Arman to the mirror.

Stunned by the reflection, Arman dropped his freshly made drink splattering Jack all over himself. Granted he was still a bit wet from the pool, and smelled like chlorine, so a shower wouldn't have been a bad idea anyway.

"What the holy mother of god?"

The glass bounced off the edge of the dresser hitting the carpeted floor, the spilled soda slowly bled across the fabric before any more words could be uttered.

In the mirror, the shadowy figure was smoking around Dustin as he sat on the bed. The reflection of this creature draped itself across Dustin's form, enveloping him into itself. Looking over to Dustin sitting casually on the bed, the view was a very different sight. The shadow hadn't materialized so it was just giddy mortal alone in his jammies. Composed and calm again. "bitch" Arman muttered terrified, then squeaking. "He's back!"

"Yeah, he is." Dustin smiled.

"Are we dying?" Arman didn't know if he or Gary or Amir had to die for this thing to show up.

"What; no! Dorkface is just a little shy." Beaming at the figure in the mirror. "You can come out, I see you." Acting all kinds of aloof.

Slowly the figure materialized alongside Dustin on the bed. Just a wisp at first, then the black gauzy form solidified slowly into the shape of a person sitting. Arman had to step back a few feet, the materialization of death was bad enough in a mirror, but in this room and in this reality? That was making it hard for the guy to breathe. Clutching his chest Dustin's friend took very deep breaths, like he was hyperventilating or something. It was all a bit dramatic as far as Dustin was concerned, so he focused on the form manifesting next to him. That, and the blood flowing to a certain spot in his neither regions.

Of course, Dustin glowed. His cheeks got rosy as his pulse raced, he looked outwardly calm as his body trembled with excitement. This person next to him after all this time, tangible and touchable.

Dustin's smile grew wider as the form materialized. The smoked hand forming flesh. Grey at first, then with hints of blue, gripped onto Dustin's hand. A welcoming handshake from an old friend, the eyes, however, held a glimmer of smitten desire within them.

The opal pupils were so dark and smoldering, downright sexy compared to any Dustin had seen before. Deep and rich, the only part of the face not covered in grey-black wrappings. Fully manifested into a corporeal form, this creature now had a physical presence that Dustin could feel, smell and enjoy in every way he could imagine. The glint in his eyes emanated such desire that the shrouded forms boney cheeks turned a darker blue-grey.

"Hello." Dustin was minutely shaky in his tone, so much anticipation came across.

"Hi." Deep and sultry in its reply. Raw sensual energy rose fast off these two bodies.

Completely shocked by the grim shade taking solid form in front of his best friend, Arman could only let out a gurgled "Yurp!" which was enough to draw the attention of those smoldering black pools that were this creature's eyes.

"Arman, hello again. Please relax." Attempting a smile under the gauze. The subtly was lost on the mortal.

"Uh, hi... So, like you're like umm, really here!" Just gawking at the form on the bed next to Dustin. "And I can see you, in our room?"

Dustin was silent, blushing so deeply, the shadow figure smushed up next to him, an arm draped behind Dustin's back, leaning in close, face to face. The taller black form, now in an ancient tattered cloak and real gauze, made subtle ruffling noises as it moved. Arman beckoned Dustin with his eyes, pleading for him to offer any kind of response, but to no avail. Dustin was as crushed out as any teen in the front row at their first concert with some lame ass popstar lipsynching some atrocious power ballad. And about as useless. Big-eyed and looking like drool would be gushing from his face any second, his body hummed at being close to this larger than life (literally) figure.

"I am. In the flesh, such as it is." It's voice smooth and sexy. Dustin could only hum hearing it.

"K." Arman simply stood there processing for a while. He was tired, a bit wet, kind of sticky from the knees down and watching a truck ton of odd. If he was thinking at all, Dustin would realize he may need a minute. "So... I'm going to go and shower because this is all a bit too much. How about you guys stay here and hang out?" Slowly bobbing his head.

"Arman, everything's okay. Go shower. I know it's late and a bit much to take in but he's a really good guy, and you'll like him if you take the time to get to know him." Dustin made a face urging his friend to be cool.

"I said the same thing to you about Gary, and look how that's going." Arman's spine slowly regrouping for another round.

"I like Gary." Dustin fained shocked, this was a good way to dispel weirdness.

"Really?" Playing as if he was intently interested.

"Yes, the same way you like a pet." Smirking.

"Um-hmm."

"Granted, someone else's pet. Like a neighbor down the street, you don't spend much time with." If Dustin was being honest. "But he's much deeper than Gary, on so many levels." Dustin poked his finger through a space between ribs. Like if there was skin.

This was becoming too odd for it not to be funny. Making it possible for Arman to deal with the situation. "Gary's deep. Not as deep as your hand in the corpse's chest, but he has depth." Pointing to Dustin with his arm nearly concealed by the rotted apparition.

"I stand corrected." Chuckling.

Arman smirked, "Dead dude obviously has way more to offer than Gary, the question is what? I'm not calling him Vid-whatever, so do you have like a real name... Or should I just call you the grim reaper?" Things were normalizing as best they could, considering.

"Oh, I hadn't thought of that. A nickname perhaps." The shadows boney hand with black bandages did a small theatrical twirl.

"More like a stage name I think. How about Maahaf?" Dustin acted so pleased with himself.

The cloaked form looming over Dustin made a shocked expression. Unseen but alluded too by the movement of its facial wraps.

"Really? Again, you bring him up. Perhaps you'd rather spend time with the ferryman, I can set you up." Pulling back from Dustin slightly. "He's single at the moment."

"No thank you. Fine, let's call you Aken. It's easy enough to pronounce." Starring death smugly in the face.

"Really? Smart ass." Was all Dustin got back in return.

"Well, if you don't like that, we could always go with Kherty." A smirk was forming on Dustin's face.

"What are you going on about?" Arman blank-faced, stared at them; so clearly lost.

"Dustin's teasing me." Pouty sounding from under his shroud. "The jest is in honor of your mother's family."

"Okay, well that's dumb. Because I don't understand who either of you are talking about, cause my mom, doesn't know squat about Egypt. And never taught me anything about any of that." Sounding snotty. Like really kind of nasally, the dip in the pool may have water logged Arman.

"I could try calling him names in Punjabi..." Dustin offered. "Like your dad used to yell at us when we stole the car."

"Funny smartass. See this, that right there, is why no one liked you as a kid." Wagging his finger at Dustin, in a very flamboyant manner.

"Well, snot, you really should blow some of that out your nose by the way. I'm not going to stroke his ego and tell everyone he's Seker. How about something we all can understand. It's just a nickname after all." Batting his lashes to the shroud. "Like Duamutef."

"Ha... Funny." The specter's tone was flat.

"Well, you do adore your mother." Sticking his tongue out, Dustin liked toying with the reaper. "My little lily flower." Blowing kisses. This was getting a bit gross for Arman.

"Perhaps I should leave, it seems you'd prefer to be with someone else." Faining it would depart, Dustin reached out grabbing the shrouds gauze bound boney hand, holding it tight in his.

"I'll stop. Please stay, I was just playing." Batting his come hither eyes at the apparition in the flesh.

"You guys are super weird." Arman just shook his head at them.

"This is just light-hearted banter. There's nothing; as you say, weird? About it." The dark eyes peered at Arman, death hoped he used the term properly.

"You have to have a heart to be light-hearted." Dustin chuckled.

"That was a tad personal. I might have to hold that against you." Rubbing his gauzy forehead against Dustin's. He pretended to scowl.

"You can hold anything against me, anytime." The lust in Dustin's voice was unmistakable, death purred at the thought of enjoying his fleshy love.

"Really? Come on guys, I'm standing right here!" Arman's stomach flipped. "And now is when you get all extroverted, in front of me? So gross."

Dustin limply let out a half-hearted "sorry" then whispering quietly to death, "I'm not sorry" taking a whiff of his wrappings. *The smell of incense and old tombs, cold and sexy.* Dustin's heart skipped a beat.

"You guys figure it out; or don't... I'm going to go hide in the shower for a bit." Sick of watching Dustin and the foggy reaper reenact the lead-up of every porno ever made, Arman backed away toward the bathroom. Thinking for a quick second before his brain melted, about one small detail. "I'm not going to trip and die or anything, am I?" A worry seeping through in his tone. "You know, slip and fall in the shower, or drown? Or a pipe will burst and smash my head in?"

Getting glares, not mean ones, but like he just asked a really dumb question, Dustin and the foggy guy in black glared at him. "Dude, this isn't some horror movie; chill." Looking sideways at his friend.

"Oh no. Arman, this is merely a social visit. I have nothing on the schedule for you for quite some time." Attempting a smile, a smile Arman wouldn't be able to see.

"Cool, cool. Good to know, you guys have fun then." Dashing into the bathroom.

"I thought he'd never leave, where were we?"

"What about...?"

"Oh who cares, we'll think of something to call you if you meet anyone. It's not often I get you alone in the flesh."

"Oh my..." Moving his boney hand to Dustin's knee, then slowly with the anticipation building up, the desiccated left hand of death took Dustin by the thigh and caressed its way up the torso. Its right arm cupping the small of Dustin's back pulling him close. This was it, no force on earth would stop this, their first kiss on the physical plane. Leaning in, the bandaged face met with Dustin's lips, as he pressed against the reaper.

Taking his grey and slate hand, the shadow pulled and pushed at the back of Dustin's head bringing him closer in to be devoured by kisses. It was on: death pushed Dustin down holding him tight, wrapping the cloak around him to make out passionately. The energy and lust from Dustin urged him on. Dustin shaking and moaning in ecstasy over this merging.

After a very long and much-needed shower, Arman returned to the main room expecting something, just not what he saw. Standing just past the door of the bathroom, near the first bed, Arman was drying off when he had to cease, struck motionless, face cringing in horror at the sight on the next bed over.

There Dustin's head was tossing and turning, moaning with grunts of lust and desire as a shrouded figure of the reaper molested his lower regions. Unable and or unwilling for the brain to discern exactly which parts were inter-joined, Arman witnessed the back of the gauzy black cloak as it seemed to be face down on Dustin's junk.

Bobbing and devouring some piece of flesh into itself, the shadow was over eager in its feast. Writhing on the bed Dustin held his arms at bay as best he could to allow this creature access to his most sacred temple.

Stunted by the sight of these events Arman had to speak out before his eyes would melt out of his head. Stuttering and aghast he attempted to approach the situation in a calm and rational manner, like any mammal being vivisected while conscious would do.

"Holy christ on a keychain! What the bejeezus is going on!?" His dark suede hue fading to a caucasian white. "You're getting a blowjob from a corpse?" Arman's stomach flipped.

"What, sorry!" Dustin opened his eyes and in a matter of a blink, the unflappable man was beet red. He was caught in the act with his supernatural lover who equally shocked, fogged around to Dustin's side. In unison, acting like two amateurs who'd just been caught doing it in the bushes in a public park, Dustin and the shade sat up straight covering their exposed regions. Acting all *'Hey, we were just sitting here...'* pretense, like nothing happened.

"Dude: What the actual fuck!?"

"Firstly, he's not a corpse, and sorry I didn't think we were going to get this far tonight." Breathing heavily and full of adrenaline, Dustin's voice was a tad shrill.

"You didn't?" The shadowy figure looked deeply in Dustin's eyes. "You had to know I've wanted to be with you. Did you not feel the same?" The longing in his voice made Dustin twitch downstairs.

"I just meant, I thought you'd want to take it slowly, get to know each other better?" He cupped the apparition's face forgetting for the briefest moment Arman was leering at him.

"I do know you; I know your very essence and being. I've longed for you from the time your energy became aware." Dustin without much care moved in for the smooches. It kind of freaked his friend out watching from the sidelines.

"Guys!" Arman's head may have actually exploded if he had to watch any more.

"Sorry... What were you saying?" Smirking, Dustin attempted to pay attention.

"That I walked in and watched death get all hot and bothered by going down on you! Not cool!" Arman had never this kind of conversation with his best friend. Or anyone, and by extension, didn't know anyone who had ever had this kind of conversation period. And yet there it was.

"Oh..." Dustin thought for a second. "I see what you did there. Death warmed over joke. Needs work but a good try. How about this? Don't think about it as getting a BJ, but as the eternal kiss?" Trying (and failing) to make light of the situation.

Scoffing at the bad humor and the snittyness from Dustin; Arman watched, possibly for the first time he had ever seen it, Dustin acting all sorts of vexed. Normally super chill, he was rattled to no end over being caught literally with pants down, nipples exposed.

"I can't handle this... Dustin, I love that you found a guy that makes you happy, but I'm really freaked out. I can't take anymore tonight." Slumping down on the spare bed, covering his face with a towel.

"Right, sorry. I get that, we'll go. You stay and rest." Pulling his jammie bottoms up fast before Arman looked at his penile area.

"I'm not trying to be a dick, I'm just sort of overwhelmed by everything. This is all new to me." Looking earnestly at Dustin, Arman tried not to make that cock block sneer.

"I'm sorry for overstepping, I will leave and let you both rest." The apparition bowed its covered cowl, causing Arman to twinge like he was being a prick. Dustin, on the other hand, wasn't about to let go that easy.

"No, you don't get enough personal time as it is." Glaring at the shroud, it acquiesced as Dustin's lust flared. Then like a lion Dustin turned his sights on his best friend. "Arman you stay and get some sleep, we'll find a place to hang out."

"I'm sorry, you guys don't have to leave. I'll sleep in the other room." Images of Gary and Amir in bed together in the next room over caused him to shiver. "Or I'll sleep in the tub."

"No, we shall go... Come o' wondrous other-kin." The grim took hold of Dustin's hand and like smoke, flared up and dissipated. Just like that, they were gone in a blaze of black haze.

Thinking the universe was just turned sideways and everything would be crashing down on him any minute, Arman found some undies and a nightshirt to throw on. Then reached for the first bottle he could grab and broke the seal.

X

At some indecent hour, the sound of a fist repeatedly striking the outside of the wooden door, combined with muffled cries denoted some nightmarish creature begging to be let in. Face down under a pillow the body of the crumpled man rumbled slowly awake to contend with whatever horrible thing was at the door.

"Guys, open up!" The sound was like shouting from inside a paper bag, low and irritating. "Anyone there?" With notes of sadness and desperation. The voice, instantly recognizable was much more annoying than the one inside Arman's hung over brain.

Taking a sideways glance at the off label bottle of wine on the bedside table Arman rose, staggered like a zombie to the other whine, his face reflecting the disgust he felt. The contents of the bottle percolating, slowly turning to vinegar from being exposed to the warm air, would likely be the murder weapon used to kill the one begging to be let in.

Yanking open the room door Arman watched Jordon stop, staring mid-knock. He was looking a bit worse for wear compared to the night before. The blue stars and stripes shirt turned inside out and wrinkled with sagging jeans riding low as if he threw them on in a hurry. Dark circles under his sad eyes. On any other day he would be laughed at mercilessly by his friends.

"Where the hell have you been!?" An intense angry shrill spilled out. "We spent most of the night trying to reach you! Why didn't you answer your phone?" Blocking the entrance until he got some response from Jordon.

"My battery died, sorry." Standing there acting oblivious to the rest of the world.

"You didn't see any of the million texts from Amir, or me, or Dustin?" Not buying it.

"I just thought Amir was being paranoid, then my phone died. It's no big deal." Looking tired and irritated by the interrogation.

"What happened to you?" Dustin's voice came from behind Arman. He turned quickly.

Lying back under the sheets on the second bed, Dustin snuggled into the body of the hottest man Arman, or for that matter; Jordon had ever seen. The man with his thick muscular arm around Dustin, pecking kisses on his head.

Jordon stopped in his tracks unable to speak due to the instant growth in his pants. The man draped around and doting on Dustin was a dark tan hue, deep smoldering eyes with curly black hair. His striking features were solid and firm. A long strong nose, wide jawline and powerful cheeks; he looked right out of an ancient statue from old. In the flesh, he was completely ripped and muscular, with just the right amount of chest hair beckoning the two men at the door to follow it down his frame. To their eyes dismay, it was covered by a sheet blocking what must be the best view they'd see in their short lives.

The silhouette under the white cotton gave the impression that it would deeply impress both men brazenly gawking. For Arman at least, the image of this Adonis was colored by the fact he'd seen what he started out as, giving his friend a gauzy blow job.

Unable to refuse the question, Jordon felt the need to share and then, if allowed to, spread his legs and stretch his hole completely for the hottie in the bed. He'd do it on a busy highway if this guy asked him. "I did a massage on my client, then he asked me to dinner. We had drinks and I passed out. I swear nothing happened!"

"Um hmmm." Arman wasn't buying it.

"Fine, I was naked when I woke up. It was part of the fantasy and I don't remember. But I made five hundred off the night." Attempting to sound defiant. Instead, Jordon came across like a nasty tramp.

"Gross, no one wants to hear about that. We spent most of the night in the hospital." Arman turned and moseyed back to the bed, landing sideways.

"I just meant, why didn't you get in touch with us? We could have used your help." Dustin realizing he didn't want all the details of Jordon's evening. This was the kind of tag-team Jordon didn't like.

"Do you still feel good about stopping him from doing something tremendously foolhardy... Twice." The studly form of the reaper smirked at Dustin.

"Let's just say I didn't want to wait around and fill out forms." Talking like Arman and Jordon weren't in the room. They certainly weren't mentally, not having any idea of this back and forth.

"You sure that was the only reason." Glaring.

"Okay fine. Amir is such a drama queen, all the crying and breaking stuff. Like my stuff, I didn't want that on this trip." Dustin sneered at the naked hunk.

"Now that, I can believe." Smiling death rewarded Dustin with a deep tongue filled kiss.

"So you're back? Is that... him?" jabbing his finger across the way, Arman's face a sideways blank canvas.

"Oh, yeah." Having to turn his attention begrudgingly. "We had the best night, ended up in front of a fire on the rug in my living room. It was so romantic." Dustin all red again.

"Isn't it a bit warm for a fire?" They left Jordon to stand at the door.

"Well, he does have a habit of chilling a room when he enters." Dustin smirked.

"Funny. So; you look a little different." Turning his attention to the eye candy cradling Dustin in his meaty arms.

"This is actually how Dustin sees me. In his heart." The solid shroud of death pursed his full welcoming lips. Arman was not immune to the charms. Gary was a dog compared to this dead hottie.

Clearing his throat before he could continue. "Explain please." Arman's voice added a pitchy inflection with his face blushing crimson, he attempted to move a pillow stealthily to cover his growing interest.

"When I manifested in corporeal form, I took the image I saw in Dustin's soul. This is the way he views me." Smiling brightly. "As our connection grew, I became this flesh."

"Um, that's sweet." Arman pulled a blanket over his midsection, the pillow wasn't working well enough.

Not being the center of attention by this new stud puppy and wanting to be split up the center like a ripe melon, Jordon was now compelled to jump in. Or if the fates were kind, on.

"Dude..." Whispering to Arman, very conspicuously. "Did you have a three-way, or is Dustin getting the sloppy seconds?" As classy as he could sound while trying to keep his volume to a peep. "Cause I'd take that sloppy second anyday."

All eyes landed on Jordon, the audacity and crassness did not escape notice. "You disgusting asshole! We can all hear you!" Arman glared at Jordon, using his flopping hand to wave at Dustin and death across on the other bed. Also glaring.

Arman's hangover hurt his face, and head, in fact, his entire body, that much was obvious by his movements. Dustin thought he looked like a strung-out marionette and would have offered to help him out, but he was naked under the covers. So he decided against such altruism.

Jordon was exacerbating the situation to the breaking point. Forcing himself to get out of the bed and stand, Arman made his way to the bar cart previously ravaged after witnessing the steamy intubation of the dead by the living. Each plodding step, like having shoes made from bricks may have been comical for Dustin to watch, but it seemed awfully painful for his friend to do. Arman ruthlessly pushed passed Jordon who's only reaction was to edge his unphased self into the middle of the room. Not for one second did he avert his eyes, lasciviously staring at the hot's guy's genital outline.

Arman snagged a bottle of rum and pineapple flavored soda, pouring them into the last unused hotel cup. Warm as there was no ice, Arman was going to get obliterated and forget he ever met Jordon. They had an ice bucket at one point, but with the whole dead guy in the pool thing, they may have left it somewhere.

Wincing at the taste of the lukewarm drink, Arman turned back to Dustin and company. "So, did you kids decide on a name yet? Just wondering what to call you before I throw up?" Slumping back over onto the bed at a snails pace. "Not because of you though."

"Dude, did you pass out drinking that cheap ass Chablis?" Dustin gestured at the gurgling bottle on the table between beds.

"Yeah, and it was warm." Making a sour expression.

"And you said I was weird...We're going with Al-Mawt." Shifting gears quickly Dustin couldn't resist beaming. The figure snuggling him tightly nodded in agreement.

"Sticking with a theme eh?" Arman raised a brow. Knowing Dustin would be a dork about it.

"Yeah; well it works."

"So um, Al; is it?" Now that he had a name, Jordon could jump into jumping on that. Considering he was completely lost by anything around him other than the guy he wanted to bone, Jordon made his best sexy stance. He was about to cross a line he could never come back from.

"How about you step up to the big leagues and hang out with me for a while?" So sincere and so completely out of place.

"Oh my god! That's Dustin's friend; you ass hat!" Arman threw a pillow at the big lumbering moron. In hindsight he should have thrown the bottle of wine, Jordon might have felt it.

Sitting up in bed, Dustin was about to make Jordon suffer in some way that would no doubt frighten Arman to the core. He didn't have to, as the reaper laughed in such a manner as to convey the absurdity of the invitation. Looking over to Dustin for clarification he whispered.

"Did this insignificant mortal make a sports reference?" Dustin smirked as he nodded, while Arman chuckled into his drink.

Jordon suddenly shrank self-consciously, a thing that was rare for him. When death responded, any hope of banging this dude would be forever dashed.

"Jordon Davenport, you are a small and tragic male. You pail in comparison to Dustin Ney in every way imaginable. I would never debase myself with the likes of one who is so mundane and mediocre. When in my arms, I hold a titan." His tone echoing with a resonance normal humans aren't able to make without the help of a voice modulator. He pulled Dustin close kissing him, while keeping a cold steely eye on Jordon, shaken and devastated.

"Damn, smackdown!" Arman adding salt to the wounds. "Nice trick with voice. Very super villain like."

"Thank you."

"Jordon, get Gary and Amir up and ready, we're leaving after we eat. Make sure everything is taken to the car, packed up, ready to go." The ice in his tone wasn't lost on the reaper or Arman.

Dustin peeved at the behavior on display by his supposed friend squinted with malice. Without a word Jordon left to the other room to deal with the new nightmare he'd walk into.

"When he sees them naked and spooning, will he still do what you told him to do?" Arman asked, genuinely curious. "And could you teach me that trick? It would come in handy with Gary."

"It would take years, so not anytime soon. But yeah he'll do whatever I tell him, that asshole totally pissed me off. Jordon's so gross. Who hits on your man in front of you? That's so tacky!" Thoroughly disgusted.

"I suspect Gary will later." Arman frowned.

Almost immediately the muffled shouting in the next room began. Jordon was carrying out his marching orders, and yet apparently wasn't happy his lover was in bed with Gary. And by the sounds of the yelling,

Amir wasn't too pleased with Jordon either. Something about staying out all night while their lives were in peril? *Here come the tears and drama.* Dustin mused at that all too familiar thought.

"I'm your man?" The solid spirit in the bed took his meaty finger and brushed back Dustin's short hair, a big smile on his face.

"In this form you are." Dustin grinned broadly. "In fact, in this body, you have all the physical traits as anyone else, and therefore are at my mercy." Pecking the studly reaper on the tip of his long thick nose.

"Eh?" Arman gave Dustin a sideways look while drinking the hangover away.

"When he takes on the physical manifestation of someone, he's flesh and blood, just like us." Dustin used this opportunity to caress the form of Mawt. For academic purposes only... "A real heartbeat, a racing pulse." His hand rubbing the grim's chest. "The sexy musky scent, and by the sound of it, a rumbling stomach."

"Seriously Dustin, stop with the molesting? That's too much for my brain to handle at the moment. Take it down a notch." Sounding a bit snippy and looking very disgusted.

He supposed he had a valid point. Dustin was lying naked in bed with death. Who was also naked, so Arman might have mixed feelings what with the newness and all.

"Yup... sorry." Removing his grabby paw.

"So he's not dead? Death is alive? I'm confused." Arman rubbed his head. His brain hurt.

"I am beyond life and death, I am. On the material plane, I have substance, like any living organism." Al, as he was probably going to be called for the rest of his time around these folks, attempted to clearly explain in terms Arman would think was logical. "I am the great equalizer. One of the forces of creation. Where there is life there is also me, no one escapes that simple fact."

"Just so you know; I'm not calling you Leveler. That would take way to long to explain the socio-political implications to our friends.

We might as well call you Cihuateteo, or the black impermanence. If you had any ideas about that." Dustin poked his finger at the beefy reaper who pursed his lips in silent acquiescence, accepting that Dustin was the one in charge. By the visible growth under the sheets, he was more than accepting of that fact.

Arman, laid there just watching, he was finding out how Dustin felt for a change. No one paying attention to him, having conversations like he wasn't in the room. Arman didn't like it.

"K. So you're not dead, cool." Inserting himself back into their reality.

"For all intents and purposes, he's like any other guy. He eats, he craps, he pants when he's excited" An 'ew' peeped from Arman. "and speaking of, when was the last time you ate?"

"The early nineteen nineties. A lovely Afghani family invited me in for a meal." The reaper grinned. It was sexy on his chiseled face. "There was so much death and dying I was noticed. They were kind and the meal was delightful." Sounding so pleased.

"Well, we're going to grab a bite before we hit the road. Would you care to join us?" Dustin begged, leering longingly into the face of his unearthly studmuffin.

"I would like that. I do have to meet with some of the others beforehand. Perhaps I can join you after?" Something was stirring in the spirit, and not just in his loins.

"Totally, we got to get up and get ready anyway."

"Then I shall see you later." Death reached in pressing his pouty lips to Dustin's, pushing his tongue deep inside his lover's mouth. After a few long moments of passionate kissing, the apparition dissolved into a haze of black smoke, dissipating away leaving Dustin alone on the bed.

Arman, of course, watched the whole thing, like watching a trainwreck. One where the person wants to look away, but they can't. He may have been able to handle it better if it wasn't for the pain. Feeling like aluminum foil slowly being stepped on, with vinegar for guts, watching the hot guy fade into a cloud of smog while frenching Dustin probably would leave some sort of mental scaring.

Choking down the faux pina colada, his face became more sour with each guzzle. "Arman, what are you doing, we should probably get ready to head out." A perky Dustin hummed.

Dustin reached for his bag over the side of the bed. Unlike Arman, he was eager to get up and get moving. Arman squinted as his head pounded like a drum. He could hear the shouting and muffled screaming from the next room as the three men who they believed were friends were arguing about the events of the previous day. Wanting nothing more than sleep or death, all hope of that possibility for Arman was dashed due to the cursing from them and Dustin acting like a bouncy child. All giddy and chipper.

"I'm trying to drink the pain away, but I think it's just making me want to throw up. Dibs on the bathroom." Arman with labored movements rose to stumble into the toilet in order to collapse in front of the porcelain god.

Reaching into a pouch Dustin pulled a vile from his bag. It was way old school one with a twist off cap. Tossing it to Arman, or close enough to Arman where he could reach for it. Moving painfully slow, he picked up the small bottle and peered at it like it was from another planet.

Dustin found a spare pair of boxers to slide on. They may be close but there was no way Dustin wanted to be naked in front of Arman. Arman wouldn't want that either. Growing up around nudists, they appreciated having certain boundaries with each other.

"Drink some of that, it'll help. But I suggest you throw up first." Digging for a shirt.

"What is it?" Arman inspected the bottle and its contents from all angles.

"Grandma Hester's hangover cure. Only use half a cap full. Use too much and you'll feel stoned the rest of the trip." Wagging his finger.

"What's in it?" Arman looked suspiciously at Dustin.

"Herbs; mostly... I have to warn you it doesn't taste that great. It's better to drink it while you're drunk."

XI

Returning from the bathroom Arman was much less hung over. In fact, he was starting to act and look like his old self, minus the contents of his stomach. The walls of the restroom being so thin, there was no escape from hearing Arman worship at the porcelain alter. Added by the muffled noise in the other room from Gary, Amir, and Jordon. Lowered from shouting to some intense sounding discussion, peppered with expletives and insults simmering it certainly wasn't a post coitus serenade by starlings Dustin would have liked. More like a toxic brew, bubbling up, ready to blow its lid any second. But thank the fates, for now the steeping was contained.

On the first bed, Arman's bag was packed and ready to go, however, on the other bed, Dustin sat absentmindedly folding and refolding his jammies, his bag open and unpacked. The look on his face showed he was deep in thought. Not about Arman puking, something else had his thoughts entangled.

It wasn't the adulate joy over the dude who dissipated in smoke, it was much more somber. Arman knew that face, Dustin didn't show it often, but when he did, it was the self-reflection that makes one take stock in their priorities.

"That stuff tastes like butt." Making small talk.

"What? Oh yeah, it's pretty nasty." Looking up from his folding. "Arman, thanks for being so cool about him. I know it was weird, and I kind of got carried away. I just hope you didn't feel... excluded." Pausing to find a word, any word that expressed Dustin's thoughts. That one may not have been the best word choice.

"Ew... I'm not having a three way with you." Smirking knowingly.

"Gross, No, you twit...You know, like you weren't left out. Today and yesterday were odd, so I just hope you weren't too freaked, or if I didn't involve you more." Clarifying with a slight sneer of disgust.

116

"I get that." Sitting on the edge of the bed. "Honestly, I got a taste of it and I didn't like it. Yesterday with Gary, last night and today with you. It doesn't feel great having people make decisions like you're not there."

"Look I'm sorry..."

"Let me finish. I got a taste of it. That shit happens to you all the time, from me and those jerks we call friends. You play it off like it's no big deal but it's got to sting. So, I'm sorry. I never wanted to feel like I took you for granted." Arman's big eyes staring at Dustin, now self-conscious.

"Wow, not what I thought you were going to say. Thank you. I never meant to take you for granted either." The sincerity of worry about some small misunderstanding, prevalent in his voice. "I got carried away, but I really like him. I may even be in love with him." And now they were back to flowery romance mush.

"We're not hugging it out." Arman pretended to vomit.

"Aw." Dustin made a faux puppy face.

"Shut up. You're so much more assertive with him around. As you should be. Do you think we should try to pass him off as normal to those bozos?"

"They're not the brightest bunch. We could just scare the shit out of them and tell the truth."

Mere seconds after Dustin spoke, the sound of breaking glass was heard next door. With the shattering came renewed shouting and screaming as the blame passed from person to person in rapid succession.

"I'll go deal with the brats." Dustin stood, he was the one who could stop their fighting and move the trainwreck into the station.

"No, you go clean up, I'll get them."

"It's not a problem, I can make them behave."

"I know, but you're glistening, and you smell a little."

"Do I?" Taking a whiff of his pits. "Oh, it's the incense."

"It smells like spice and charcoal. Possibly... I want to say palm trees and something..."

"Cardamom. That and a splash sandalwood and palm fronds. You don't like it?"

"It kind of smells like, what I imagine a tomb would smell like. Or an old library?"

"You never did spend any time at the library in school, so I guess you wouldn't know what they smell like."

"Brat!"

"Sorry." Dustin made a fake frowny face with the big eyes. The aroma was an after effect of lovemaking, so to speak. "It's true though..." In a whisper.

"Best if you go shower." Arman snidely commanded, smelling the aromatic wafting of post intercourse fragrances emanating and being insulted was a tad much. "Besides, I've got some pent-up anger I want to let out." Smiling again, Arman prepared, taking a deep breath as he stormed into the next room slamming the door behind him.

A much more chipper Dustin headed for the toilet to clean up. It was late in the afternoon already so best get fueled up and head out onto the open road. *Fun* but it most likely wouldn't be.

The walls in the bathroom being thin it was easy enough to hear clearly everything in the next room "What the hell guys!" Arman shouted upon entry. "It looks like a disaster area in here." Immediately Dustin's mood continued to improve.

While in the room, "I was trying to get them up and they're being dicks!" Jordon jumped to attention receiving glares from both Gary and Amir, mostly clothed. Amir at least was wearing underwear and a tee-shirt, Gary just briefs and socks.

"Seriously, all three of you have been acting like spoiled children this whole trip! It's less than an hour before we have to check out, and you asses are breaking shit?" Arman had plenty of reason to be mad.

Gary ponied up with his warmest suck up face. He was going to grovel like the best of them. "Babe, look I'm really sorry about last night. I screwed up, I did, and we're trying to get ready but these guys won't stop fighting."

"Us? You're the one bitching about breaking your arm and nobody giving a shit!" Amir wasn't about to let Gary pawn off blame. "It was your own damn fault!"

"Guys stop!" Arman was done. "I don't care475

` 1 and I'm starving. Here's what's going to happen. Get your shit packed and get ready to head out. We're getting on the road after we eat. Is that understood?" In his mind, he was clear, with little room for interpretation. Dustin meanwhile sang to himself softly, enjoying the harsh discipline rightfully being served up.

"Arman relax. It's all okay, we'll handle it. Why don't you go get yourself a snack and wait for us? We'll just stay one more night and start fresh in the morning. That way, we can all calm down and talk about what happened yesterday."

"He asked for it now..." Dustin murmured, thinking of course, Gary decided to act like the big dog. *Big mistake, big!*

Arman seethed with anger. "Gary: Dustin, who has paid for everything on this trip, without as much as a thank you from any of you; and I, are going downstairs to eat, check out, and leave in *my* vehicle. You three can find your own way home!" Taking a deep breath, before the finale. "You guys stay as long as you want, pay for the damages to the room... And Gary, when you get back to Scranton find a new place to live! I'm done with this."

Arman determined, returned to the other room to gather up his stuff, leaving Gary annihilated in his wake. The main suite was silent, Jordon still being compelled to continue his task until he was set free, packed up the bags and began hauling them down to the SUV. Amir not sure why Jordon was doing that, helped. If for no other reason than he didn't want to be around Gary as his world crashed down around him. Amir and Jordon would need to talk, but at this moment the scene was too toxic and Amir knew better than to be in the middle of it.

Slowly a red-faced Arman tried to calm himself on the bed, scrolling through the messages on his phone. Spending a few minutes reading them he didn't hear Gary slink into the room and stand there. Left alone, ignored for several minutes this red puffy-faced man, sad and depressing waited as long as he could hold it in.

With the argument concluded, Dustin finished up in the restroom and dressed slowly at the door. He heard the silent squeak of Gary move in behind Arman. There way no way he'd warn him, this would be too funny, so he waited quietly. Dustin believed that a normal person, or normal people, would generally make themselves known, or wait until the person they were attempting to make peace with calmed down.

However, Dustin didn't really know any normal people. If Gary was considered a normal person and was an average of what most people were like, then he felt the world was doomed. He also wondered why then, were he, and his family considered odd, if Gary or any of them were normal? Chances were, Gary was just more out on a limb than he was.

This poor dumb creature, couldn't just be patient. Dustin knew this was the moment his heart would get smashed and he wanted to hear every bit of it break.

Clearing his throat finally, Gary got Arman's attention. Startled that Gary walked in, looked up in surprise. "Holy shit?"

"Arman, please. Let's talk."

"Gary stop. I'm angry, I've been angry with you since we left. You've treated me like a child and frankly, you've treated Dustin far worse."

"What's this have to do with Dustin?" The hammer was about to fall.

"Gary, none of this would have been possible without Dustin. He made sure you didn't overdose last night, checked you into the hospital *and* is paying for your wrist. Do you think we could afford the bill?" Gary's face was blank, he honestly hadn't thought about it. "He got you out of the bar and into the cab, back here and we brought you guys to the room. Dustin's been a great friend to all of us, and you treat him like he doesn't exist. And last night you did it to me."

"Babe, I never meant to..."

"I know... That's the problem. You don't think about anybody but yourself. You never have. It doesn't cross your mind that what you do has implications for other people."

"I'm sorry. What can I do, I don't want to lose you. Arman, I love you." Getting misty, Gary soldiered on. "Please, there's got to be something I can do?"

"Gary, you have to figure that out. You don't appreciate people, even your friends. Have you ever once said thank you to Dustin for anything? He's footing the bill for this entire trip, and have you even thanked him?"

"I'm sure I did."

"Not once. If you can treat Dustin like you're doing him a favor for being in your presence, what's that say about us? About you as a person? Or me, for being with a person like that?"

"I don't know..." Now crestfallen.

"That's something. Go pack up and get ready to go. Meet us in the restaurant next door when you're done. We'll go do the checkout." Arman picked up his bag and headed out to the hallway for dramatic effect, slamming the door. Instantly he turned to listen at the door, not knowing Dustin was doing the same at the other door.

Hearing Gary wander back into the other room, Arman dropped his bag at the door and sneaked back in, closing the adjoining door to wait for Dustin.

Dustin quietly opened the door and slipped out. Finding Arman back in the room checking to see if he left anything behind, Dustin put his finger to his lips, grabbed his shoes and bag up in his arms, both slipping out to head down to the lobby.

On the stairwell out of earshot from the guys. "That was such a thrill, I should break up with Gary more often!" A spiteful glee on his face.

"I heard what you said to Gary. I really appreciate it." Dustin's cheeks were rosy.

"Don't let it all go to your head, I was being selfish too. Some things came into perspective, and now I don't mind moving on." Heads lowered as they meandered down the winding stairs.

"We should prepare ourselves for an uncomfortable lunch." Dustin kind of hoped the guys wouldn't show up.

"Especially with your boyfriend coming." Knocking Dustin's shoulder with his, slight dread in Arman's face.

"Should we just go home?" Dustin could always fly out when he figured out what to tell his parents about his job.

"Dustin, you of all people know that's not an option. Your mom will make us show up, the question is, will the guys be going with us?"

"That's true." Exhaling deeply, he felt they were trapped.

"That reminds me, while you were in the shower I got a text from Alyssa. About you."

"Your sister? What's she want?" Dustin looked at Arman, this was a curious twist.

"She got the idea that you've gone missing and your parents are super worried." A knowing scowl on his brow.

"That's low, even for them! Alyssa lives in Scarsdale. Why would she know anything about anything? Also, it's not like Marta isn't tracking the credit card transactions, she knows exactly where I am." Dustin's now emanating mild frustration. He deadpan look got up and walked out the room, replaced with irritated discomfort.

"That's messed up dude. I can totally believe your mom would do that, but tracking you is one step beyond." Expressing empathy masquerading as shock.

"You didn't respond, did you?" Eyebrow raised.

Questions spooled in Dustin's head. What was his mom's plan? If even by accident Arman responded, it would unleash a cascade chain reaction that would send a tornado in a trailer park into a jealous shame spiral.

"No, after the last twenty-four hours, I figured it best to talk to you about it first."

"Good and thank you. Don't respond, Nate and Marta have gone way too far this time. I'm going to have to be as truthful and tough as you were with Gary... I just don't want to have to do it." He whimpered slightly.

"Why not? Your mom's invading your privacy and dragging other people into the drama for what? To find out you got fired!"

"Yes, precisely. Then she'll convince me to come home and date one of her friends, and I'll be trapped in that damned store, selling crystal jewelry and bath salts to tourists until I die." Dustin made his sad puppy face. Bleak and dire-looking. It was sincere enough to pose further inquiry.

"By convince; do you mean the voice thing? Like you'll have no choice?"

"Kind of. Sort of... yes. My mom will make me into a puppet." Partially joking, but partially not.

"Damn Dustin. You make your mom out to be a cartoon villain. She's really a great person." Time for Arman to drop the curtain on this melodrama.

"I know, my mom's amazing and awesome. She just gets so overprotective when she thinks something's wrong." They were almost at the lobby.

Dustin's mom was putting the squeeze on him hard, and for what? Some petty information. He kept one small event from his family, so what would happen when he dropped the bombshell about his new and budding romance? As a plan was forming in Dustin's twisted brain a spiteful smile formed on his otherwise calm face.

"This is like when we used to have soup show up at our dorm right before getting sick." Arman reminisced. "Or when..." Rambling on as the wheels turned in Dustin's mind.

There were no other people in the lobby, no staff, and no guests. The closest individual they could see was way off in the restaurant attached to the hotel. There wasn't much of a late afternoon crowd or a crowd of any sorts, a stray person here and there, blurred by the dark partition. The best they could do for the time being was wait.

"I'd forgotten about that. I suppose that's what we got for staying out partying for days at a time." Chuckling, he really hadn't paid much attention to what his friend had said, so he played it off. Arman didn't seem to notice.

"Well, you are her only child, and she worries about her little man." Arman teased.

Sneering. "Funny jackass. I just need to set some boundaries. I'll talk to them soon. I have a plan forming that'll shut them down. And it'll give me a chance to reprimand them for butting into Alyssa's life." Waiting semi-patiently at the front desk for the attendant.

"Really?" Arman was intrigued. He wasn't about to ask, because he wouldn't understand it, but he was intrigued. "That'll be an interesting conversation."

"Oh yeah, with like twenty other people listening in. Bunch of nosy monsters." Grumbling slightly.

"Is the place in New Mexico like the old one, with like a million people coming and going at all hours?" Arman made his scrunchy face. Puckered lips, and squished up nose.

"Worse... You know they moved the entire house down to the foundation, so picture a block party inside the Winchester mansion with a bigger yard. That'll be a calm night." Dustin's face showed he wasn't overjoyed by the situation. "The only thing they didn't ship was the pool, so instead, now there's an indoor arboretum. Thankfully at the apartment, we have locks." Making crazy eyes. Wide and unstable.

Arman missed the calm unflappable Dustin who never revealed any details about the happenings around him. Dustin was always the eye of the storm for Arman. If he was unphased, Arman could believe there had to be a logical reason for every weird thing that went on in their lives.

Late night food that hadn't been ordered showing up at the most auspicious times. The myriad of miscellaneous people at the Ney house coming and going, acting as if they knew company was coming. The pool parties, or any of the lavish parties that seemed to happen on a whim. The countless times they committed felonies and got off with warnings. The weird strays camped out at the Ney house for Dustin's parents to play matchmaker for... If Dustin was calm, it could all be explained as rational. Arman believed that, he was wrong.

This open and expressive Dustin was causing trepidation. Too many new and strange things had already happened, and what was to come may be odder still. Perhaps that was the reason for inviting Gary, Jordon, and Amir. Lambs for the slaughter? A buffer zone perhaps. All the batshit crazy became real, now that Dustin's deadpan gaze showed cracks.

The crows, the cat, the weird dead people. Dustin's dead, not dead boyfriend, who apparently had no name or a bunch of names, Arman had no clue, that was an inside thing. Arman was unsure about a lot of things, and yet he asked, Dustin answered, no take backs now.

"Well, that's just nifty." Confused much more than he was only moments ago.

Before they became too impatient waiting, some generic twenty-something dude walked out from the back room stirring his coffee. He didn't appear to care how long they'd stood there, or care about anything really. This attendant was just another standard-issue day worker in a blue dress shirt, looking glassy eyed as if they were dragging their ass through life.

"Sorry for the ..." Yawning. "Wait. Um, hum." He cleared his voice, trying to get it together. The steaming mug of coffee set to the side was his tell, he'd just woken up. Hair out of place, the younger male looked a bit haggard, perhaps still a tad hungover. The smell of chlorine and stale booze hinted he may have been at the pool party the night before.

"Caaaannnn..." Yawning mid-word. "I help you?" Forget hungover, he may have still been drunk.

As transactions went, everything was seamless. The signing of the statement, agreement to be billed for any additional charges, like damage and cleaning. That sort of thing.

"What if the guys get all pissy before we leave?" Arman queried. "And make more of a mess."

Dustin answered Arman with one word and slited eyes with a tense lip that spoke volumes on who would ultimately be paying for any disaster left in their wake. "Whatever..." No secret society, deep state mystery, it was all being paid for by Dustin's mom.

When finished with bed-head the two headed into the dining room next door. Upon entry, they saw the bar, small compared to many they'd been at, only room for one person at a time behind it. Not the widest selection but Dustin's eyes went immediately towards the one bottle he couldn't resist.

"Dude, they have Snake Venom!" Directing Arman to a bottle of whiskey tucked in the back behind a dusty bottle of vermouth on the top shelf, almost out of reach. Almost.

"How'd you even see that up there, it looks like they're trying to hide it." Gazing curiously.

"I could spot that bottle anywhere." Beaming, he looked squarely at the cauliflower nosed bartender. "We'll need four shots of that!"

If the crusty bartender had eyes made of knives he'd have slashed Dustin repeatedly in the face. Wincing and wheezing, the haggard man in a red vest, reached for it moving several other containers out of the way, dust and particulates falling here and there. Once down he poured the shots, leaving the dust to settle over the space. Grumpy, perspiring in the air conditioning, with nicotine stained fingers this wrinkled queen from yesteryear was about to demand payment, and possibly a human sacrifice by the look on his mug, didn't have need to as Dustin slapped Marta's black card down and said "add twenty for yourself." Changing the bartender's mood entirely.

"Dustin what in god's name is it?" Looking at the amber muck in the shot glass. "I've never heard of this snake venom shit."

"I don't think they make it anymore. I've only seen it at my parents, and grandma Hester's farm. She and granny Lucy drank it on their anniversary. And when she passed, grandma Hester kept up the tradition." Holding up the shot, waiting, waiting longer...

Guzzling back the dusty whiskey, Arman wretched. "That's disgusting!" Wincing. This was a day of bad choices apparently.

"It's an acquired taste." Making a similar stink face while choking out his words.

"It's worse than that butt hangover cure." Sneering as Dustin moved the second shot in his path.

"Come on, for my grandma's?" Dustin used his big begging eyes and puppy dog brow.

"Fine." Taking the shot.

Both soon realizing, it wasn't any better than the first. If anything it was worse. It was like the first shot seared away the lining of their mouths like acid, so the second one could stab at the nerves. Daring each other to see who would swallow first, they held the liquor in their mouths, until with eyes tearing up, Dustin and Arman finally clinched their pucker holes and guzzled it back like old pro's. Winning together, or losing together, depending on who was asked.

Several minutes later when they stopped retching from disgust, Dustin led Arman to a table near the front wall. It was out of the way with ample room to see their surroundings. The guys would find them eventually, and Dustin's friend could find him anywhere so they waited, perusing the small menu and their nightly specials. Not too many options, probably a small kitchen, but there was enough choice for a decent meal.

By the signage at the entrance, there had been a continental style breakfast they (thankfully) missed. A host of shellfish and salmon, bokchoy and breakfast burritos, with kale smoothies and banana pancakes. A strange mix of culinary experiments not normally known to go well together for the first meal of the day. Or perhaps, any meal.

The server made their way over, Sharron by the tag. They had a deep voice, and the same red vest and white shirt as 'grumpy' the bartender.

"Who knew this place was fancy enough for uniforms?" Arman whispered in a mocking tone.

"Going by everything we saw so far, I wouldn't go call this place fancy in any way." Dustin whispered back.

Sharron gave them the obligatory water, which was gone in a flash, they had some bad tastes that needed to be washed away.

The server sported a short fluffy brown and amber fauxhawk, with streaks of cerulean blue and deep purple throughout. Long multicolored nails, with glittery tips, a broad chest and slim hips. Sharron wore a big, fake as all get out, jovial smile on their sanguine lips. They had that look server's attempt to hide, yet never can quite cover up. The one of "this is some bullshit" counting mentally, every paltry cent they'd earn for having to run their ass off on a slow night.

Dustin understood the look, one that said they'd get service, but not great service. He was okay with that, it would add to Gary, Jordon and Amir's discomfort, making meeting Al-Mawt less of a jolt. Or, he thought, it would send them over the edge of reason altogether. Either way was fine.

So, like any two dudes light in the loafers on vacation, Dustin and Arman ordered the biggest fruity drinks they could get. Turned out they were in luck. To go along with the nautical themed breakfast, this no named eatery inside this tacky hotel, offered fish bowl specials on certain drinks.

Small plastic fishbowls like the ones kids used to toss ping pong balls into to win goldfish. The only real prize at all those school fundraisers, church carnivals and suburban racketeering rings was that the winner got to keep a hunk of plastic because the traumatized fish always died the next day.

This place just seemed to know how to make use of that plastic, proper like. The two sat and chatted amongst themselves for the fifteen or so minutes while they waited on the guys to make their way in.

It was a good start for the evening, but in no way would they be able to make a night out of these sweet drinks. Dustin and Arman would be tossing their sugar cookies if they continued with them. As they were ready for a second round of something different, the guys slinked in. Sullen and aggravated, the three men were silent; sitting opposite two bouncy friends not remotely bothered by the angsty-emo crew taking their seats.

Jordon looked squarely at the two across from him, hands on the table, his back straight waiting to eat like a good puppet on a string. Amir took a seat two spots down, a scowl on his mug, almost snarling. His glaring eyes toward Jordon, anger in his heart. It didn't appear as though they worked things out. Then there was Gary, moping like a puppy that got swatted for pissing on the carpet, slinked to the middle chair, sitting quietly. His body listless and shunted inward.

"Oh, this isn't going to be uncomfortable at all!" Arman exclaimed ironically.

"Is the truck packed up?" Dustin asked Jordon who perked right on up.

"Everything's packed and ready to go." Answering in flat uniformity with glares from Amir and Gary.

"Good, thank you." Dustin's voice was like a key freeing Jordon from the command. He exhaled deeply.

"So, what's the plan?" Arman looked at the three men intently.

"What do you mean, we thought you guys were going to split, then Jordon packed everybody's stuff." Amir began with Arman the turned on Jordon. "And why were you being a total dick about rushing us?"

"I don't know. I just had to make sure we were ready." Defensive and confused sounding, Jordon acting completely at a loss of what was going on.

"Anyway... Are you guys coming with us, or not?" Arman butted in, only to get them on the same page.

"Are we?" Gary peeped out, a tender sort of mousy look in his face. It might have been a pleading look, but no one had ever seen Gary plead for anything other than sex.

Begging, yes... Many times they had all seen Gary begging, and whining. But that was also for sex; the kind of begging that made most folks feel like they were in a workplace harassment video. Still, this was different. Almost like he was feeling genuine emotions other than lust, so for him, this was unusual, for Dustin it was a touch off-putting.

"You can, but there's got to be some ground rules. No fighting and stop being dicks." Not his best list, but Arman gave it a go. "And maybe show some appreciation." Emphasizing that last one.

"About that. Dustin, it's been made clear to us that we may have taken you for granted on this trip. Thanks for bringing us, and I'm sorry." Amir made a heartfelt attempt and came across sounding almost sincere.

Dustin had known Amir the longest of the three, and like Gary and Jordon, he didn't like having his flaws shared with the world. The hateful teasing between him and Gary was in its own way, their thing. However, when other people pointed out their many faults, their nerves became prickly like a roid-rage fueled cactus. He'd met Amir trying to pick up Arman, when that failed those two became friends, and Dustin always felt he was viewed as someone who clung on to Arman for popularity, which was what Amir did but would never admit. Dustin wanted to believe they were better friends than that, but the reality settled in for him long ago.

"Not a problem." Responding with a breath of coldness in his tone.

"Well, now that's all settled." Arman picked up the menu hiding his face, whispering to Dustin "awkward!" while making big bug eyes. Dustin struggled to keep a straight face.

The server made their appearance not too long after, a good thing too. The group was getting restless. Well, at least the three men who got their feelings hurt. Dustin merely smirked while they fidgeted in their seats.

"Um, does anyone want anything from the bar?" They asked, not looking like they wanted to get too close to the group.

"Oh yes, I think we're definitely going to need drinks." Dustin relied robustly. "Cosmo for me."

"Agreed, same…" Then Arman and in short order around it went.

"Gin and tonic…"

"Vodka soda…"

"Whiskey rocks, a double…" Finally, from Amir sounding curt.

"Alrighty, then…"

The server hastily backed away. It was as if there was a dark cloud hanging over the table. However, Dustin knew he was waiting in the wings to make his appearance. The sneak wouldn't show himself until the opportune moment and Dustin wasn't about to beg him, at least not yet.

<h1 style="text-align:center">XII</h1>

Attempts were made at small talk, not terribly well but were being made. The overall vibe was one where there was going to be a détente of sorts. To try and take the edge off.

"Oh, a salmon mousse." Jordon, looking at a specials menu peeped out meekly.

Scanning the room, Dustin very casually checked out what the five other people eating were having. Two sets of couples and a single gentleman were all the other diners in the place. One of the couples was consuming that special, and without trying, Dustin noticed blue sparks popping off it. A clear indication it had gone bad. His attention focused back to the table, he was hungry and wanted to keep his appetite.

"Gary." Arman spoke his name and he stopped everything, listening with rapt attention. "It's probably best if someone else drives the rest of the way. The doctor said not to overdo it on your wrist."

"Oh... Okay." Gary's face turned red looking hopeless.

Turning to Dustin. "Wow, this is going well." Smirking like someone who was just about to open Pandora's box.

Before Dustin could respond, some old habits reared their ugly faces. "What did you expect? These guys are asses!" Amir barked at Gary, however, most of his ire was directed in Jordon's direction. "Arrogant shits, think the world revolves around them."

"You're one to talk!" And it started. Gary visibly upset and now had an opening. "It's not like you didn't have a role in this." Wagging his cast around the table. It wasn't all that clear on what he was referring to.

"I didn't do anything!" Amir contended.

"No, you just bitched and moaned. You could have put your foot down and stopped him."

Jordon was turning red. "Gary; shut the hell up! You two were in bed together, you don't get to criticize anyone!"

It seemed the reason Jordon was upset with the other two was now revealed. Surprised for a change, Dustin now believed Jordon had a jealous streak, in a double standard sort of way. But it did exist.

"Nothing happened!" Amir talking across Gary to Jordon. "You'd have known that if you weren't out whoring around all night!" The venom in his voice was palpable. Dustin and Arman watched in delight.

"Guys!" Arman About to speak what might have been a profound statement was interrupted, as all the phones in the restaurant began ringing at once. Dustin instantly tensed up, ready to spring into action. Louder and louder, Arman's, Gary's all five diners in the place. Even back at the bar where the server and bartender wanted no part of the table of angry Mo's.

"Fuck me." Under his breath, then bellowing. "No one answer that!" His fingers pointed, moving to each person now frozen in place, unable to answer that damned noise.

Everybody in the room was feeling compelled to say hello, yet Dustin, used every bit of effort he could muster to hold them off from doing so. Arman was warned weird would happen, just not this kind of weird. So his look of astonished awhjuynsde was justified. Dustin however, was sort of feeling Arman was enjoying this/ a tad too much and wanted to bop him in the nose. Taking the high road instead he held out his hand asking(ish).

"Gimmie your phone... Please." He acted more than happy to comply, almost snorting in laughter.

Answering, all the other devices ringing went silent. The blank confused stares however continued. "Mom, dad! What's the matter with you?"

Awaiting a response, hearing it, then he laid into them. "It wasn't remotely necessary. As if I'd tell those three anything personal. They're idiotic, reckless, self-obsessed, ego-driven twits. And Arman wouldn't say anything!" Some garbled rumbling on the other end. "Anymore than having the men's group or the coven listening in on the call?"

Amir was the only one of the three men opposite to change his expression to a scowl, like he knew he'd been insulted. Dustin of course thought justifiably, so he really didn't pay heed to the scowl. He did notice the bewildered stares on Jordon and Gary's faces. But just for a moment though, he had more pressing matters to contend with at the moment and thought it'd sink in eventually.

"Did he say coven?" Gary leaned in whispering to Arman who just shrugged his shoulders.

"Because I can hear Ammogene and her three pack a day wheezing. And Nate; Mister Simmons is touching himself again!" Some garbled reply. "He's a perv dad! He needs to be on a watchlist." More clattering.

The other men at the table leaned closer to listen with an air of mild fright taking hold on them for the scenario they were witnessing.

"Marta no. Do not use that voice with me!" After a second or so, of more garbled squawking on the other end. "I've had a lot of practice on the trip, that's how. Get everyone off the phone... And don't you dare let the coven invoke, or else!"

The vein on Dustin's temple throbbed, he was visibly mad. Arman, in fact, none of them had ever seen that before. It looked really out of place.

"Yup, he said coven..." Arman said as Gary just blinked. Then leaning into Dustin's ear he whispered "you alright?" Dustin's cheeks were puffing a rosy color.

Dustin nodded, thankful for Arman's empathy, but understanding how he in no way wanted to get involved. Dustin himself didn't want to be involved either, but it was his family.

"Mom, Nate. Where's Hester?" Leaning over to whisper to Arman. "Grandma will rein them in..." Except. "What do you mean she's on a date? With who?" His face turned sour, tongue out gagging quietly to Arman.

"Who is it?" Quietly.

"Nancy Shullwalter." His eyes narrowed. Arman shook his head, not recognizing the name. "Mrs. Henley, she reverted back to her maiden name after the divorce."

"Our guidance counselor from high school? Yuck!" Arman bellowed. "Does she still have those hideous figurines?" Arman couldn't keep from asking.

More garbled chatter on the other end. "She's been going on about them nonstop. Hester's so bored she's bailing." It seemed a topic of gossip at the Ney household when this conversation began.

"Wait, how's she on a date with Henley? Did the old bag move?" Deep concern frosted his face.

"Hester's in Scranton." Frowning at the thought of his grandmother and their high school guidance counselor. They never liked her much. She spent so much time trying to catch them in the act of causing mischief, which, even though they were, Dustin knew she wouldn't catch them. He just found it annoying that she didn't give up and move on with her life.

"You were just there, she didn't call?" Back and forth stares from the other side of the table, like toddlers trying to follow tennis. Arman seemed to be rolling with it pretty well for the most part.

"She, unlike my parents... Lets me have some privacy." A loud harrumph on the other end. "It's true though, you're butting in, just as we sat down to eat. And for what? Because I wanted to wait to tell you some news until I decide what *I* want to do!" Louder rumbling. "When's she getting home?"

Dustin made a few "uh huh's" hearing the rabble on the other side. "No one's ordering the salmon mousse!" Expelling his breath, he wasn't about to get sidetracked. "Yes I know it's turned. Not the point! Marta, why would you involve Arman's sister? She lives in Scarsdale for goddess sake!"

He waited while she explained, doing a bunch of nodding and eye rolling while Arman held his ear as close to the phone as he could.

"That's stupid. You guys knew exactly where I was..." He was cut off. "No... Don't send a raven. We'll be in Santa Fe before it gets out of the state." Dustin was becoming exasperated.

Jordon leaned into the others to ask "do either of you understand any of this?" waving his hand at Dustin, while Arman held his ear up alongside him.

"Not a word." Gary was blank faced. Amir nodded and shrugged.

"If you behave yourselves and stop being so damn nosy, I may share some news with you..." The voices on the other end jumped on that. "Well, I'm not going to tell you what it is, I said I might!"

Prattling went on for a little while longer, with Dustin occasionally making the "uh-huh" or "nuh-huh" grunts here and there. It appeared there was a larger discussion in the background happening on the other end. He just kept thinking how his family needed to get their own lives, outside of the house. This was all a bit much.

"Nate, Marta; relax. I'm old enough to make my own decisions and you just have to accept that. We'll be out there in a couple of days. Nate, you should get ready, the guys need a total work over, they're really screwed up." Dustin stared at the three opposite. They took on that deer in headlights gaze. "Yeah, hot messes. Every one of them needs total body realignment."

After more rumbling and grumbling on the other end, the conversation died out. "See you guys soon, behave..." The phone went quiet as Dustin looked over to Arman, "that went well."

"That was painful, but like watching a car crash in slow motion, painful." Smirking.

"It was, and thank you smart ass. And I was wrong, it wasn't twenty people. It was over thirty listening in."

"Why?" Was about the only thought Arman could express.

"Nate's entire men's group was on the line." Rolling his eyes back into his head.

"Ew."

"Um-huh." Dustin swigged back his drink ready for another round. "At least Hester will be home tonight, she can knock the crazy out of em." Taking a much needed meditative breath.

"Good to know. Anyway, Dustin how's your grandmother getting home?"

"Flying..." Responding with some, *how else would an old lady get around* snotty attitude.

"How's she flying?" Snotty tone back at him, it was like they were in grade school again.

"On a plane."

"No shit! It just seems a bit much to fly out to Scranton for a date, and fly home later the same night!" Arman sounding a scoche huffy.

"Oh that... Hester's got tons of family who work for airlines. She travels all over for next to nothing. It kind of sucks for the rest of us." Pretending to scowl.

"You're stupid... And here I always thought she was like some big wig. Rushing around on important business." Arman's idea of Dustin's super cool grandmother now appeared to be a tiny bit tarnished.

"No, she's just an old lady with too much free time and a penchant for hook-up apps and booty calls." Dustin was matter of fact about the whole thing.

"Ew..."

XIII

Handing Arman back his phone Dustin was a little red in the cheeks. A sign the alcohol and his parents were affecting him. "Thanks. Do you still have the elixir on you by chance?"

"That butt tasting drink? Yeah. So, I'm guessing that's why you kept your phone off." Arman pulled the bottle out and passed it to Dustin, he instantly took a swig of it making a major stink face.

"Yup. Battery out and buried in my desk at home."

"Is it safe if I use more of that, I kind of want to get plastered?" Arman had the impression the night was going to get even stranger and wanted to be ready.

"You probably shouldn't, or you might start acting like they were last night." Eyeing Gary and Amir, who were becoming agitated for some reason, by the look on their faces.

"Oh, yeah no..." Arman was going to ask some follow-up questions however some others beat him to it.

"What the hell was all that?" Amir was first to pipe up. A bit demanding, but he wanted answers.

"What did you mean by a coven? Like a real one; you know like in the movies, and with the people, and those hats?" Gary hesitated using the actual word, like if he said it, he'd have to put money in the swear jar.

"Witches, yes." Dustin looked Gary up and down like the man was stupid. He was acting a fool the whole trip so it was to be expected. "I grew up in a family of witches, and?"

"Your family is a bunch of witches... that explains A LOT!" Arman had some pieces come together in a snap. He wasn't truly shocked about the revelation, snorting before he could stop himself.

"Not all of them, some are sages, or seers, or animists; others are just kind of wyrd. I thought you knew that... It *was* kind of obvious." Smirking at his friend. "My cousin Kendra's psychic."

"Well; now it's obvious!" Arman sucked his ice. He felt like laughing, the other three did not.

"So, like do you all..." Dustin knew exactly where Gary's question was going and wanted no part in it.

"I'm gonna stop you right there... We're not doing the whole twenty questions thing! You don't know anything, and what you think you know is wrong and anything you'd ask is going to be a NO. Because you're ignorant. I mean, let's face it, collectively; you three are unbelievably sheltered from pretty much everything!" Wagging his finger at them, Dustin was done pussyfooting around the alphas.

"That was hateful!" Jordon sniped.

"Is it though?" Arman sniped back. "I mean, come on... Have any of you even read his last book?"

"You wrote a book?" Amir was proving the point.

"Really guys? Do any of you have any idea what Dustin even does for a living?" Not that Arman did either, but he at least tried to understand what ethnographic anthropology was. The others hadn't.

"You're an art teacher? Right?" Amir attempted.

"No." A sour response from Dustin's sour face.

"Volleyball coach?" Gary's attempt, which got glares from every other person at the table.

"Really Gary? And you wonder why I want to break up with you!" Arman was losing his patience, and if the server didn't come by sometime soon he'd lose his buzz.

"You were serious about that?" Now deflated, Gary slumped.

"Yes! Yes, Gary I was, you're a selfish prick! Do you even have a clue about what I do for work?" This was a trick question, seeing as Gary had been to Arman's work on many occasions.

"no..." He said meekly. Sad, but honest.

"I hate you."

Gary was saved from an ego trampling belittlement for a short while as Dustin's date finally revealed himself. Now that it was safe to venture into plain sight, his phantasmagorical form fluttered into reality. He'd been lurking in the shadows, this shadow, however now fully showing himself to the patrons and staff at that moment.

The specter fogged into the dining area with black smoke dissipating from its tethered frame. Dressed smartly in a black button-up, wearing a tight tailored pair of black slacks, this sultry spectral manifestation materialized behind the three men opposite Dustin.

Glowering that this fab phantom didn't appear sooner; when he could have used a saving, the sexy spirit moseyed around to meet Dustin in an embrace. This action caught Gary and Amir off guard. Jordon scoured as he recognized the stud that turned his balls indigo and toppled the pedestal his ego once called home.

Arman had to admit, clothed, this guy was smoking. Also, because he had saw actual smoke as he entered into reality, he understood that he wasn't a real person. At least looked like any real person he'd ever met. The image of a bandaged skeleton flashing across his mind allowed Arman to better handle the sight before him.

Gary and Amir weren't so fortunate. Amir became super jealous, some hottie to draw Jordon's attention, and Gary could deal with this guy, looking roughly the same age (yet much more attractive) if he had some squealing youngin inbetween him and the dude he wanted to rub his junk against.

"Took you long enough to show yourself." Reaching up, Dustin was pulled deeply into an embrace, the living flesh of death held him tightly.

"It was just so painful to listen too, I didn't want any part of that conversation." Kissing his lover deeply and passionately as the server stood a few feet away waiting to approach.

"Um huh, come on, park it." Not having it, Dustin motioned the sensual creature to have a seat. It did so, so smoothly, almost like smoke, with billowy wisps trailing off. Gary seeing tracers of disappearing black smog was uncertain if it was the after effect of being high, or the man was indeed smoldering. Either way, the stud in black paid no heed to the streaming trails and took a seat.

After getting situated and taking ample time to caress Dustin's face with his strong supple hands, the spirit made ready to play nice with the mortals present. "Mr. Davenport, it's decent to see you again." The coldness present in his tone.

"Sup." Jordon became uncomfortable instantly and squirmed slightly. Reminded by the steely tone, he wasn't in any way, shape or form considered a playmate for the hottie across the table.

The thought stung harder than he would have liked and it showed, his ears turning beet red. Amir perked up watching the attractive male only begrudgingly acknowledge Jordon who was unused to people not wanting him. This man's face glowed however, when he looked on Dustin, even if only for a second.

"Mr. Winslow, Mr. Farahani, it is a pleasure to make your acquaintance." Pleasant, with all the formality of a funeral setting. "Arman, hello again." Much livelier.

"Hey. You look good with actual clothes on." Toasting the guy with his empty, rattling it a touch to signal the server for another.

"Hello..." Gary eyed this guy up and down, Arman having already met him, but watching the guy react to Dustin, if he were a cartoon Dustin thought giant question marks would be sprouting from his head. "You guys met?"

"Yeah, he's a friend of Dustin's; obviously." Arman pointed to the fact that the apparition would not stop massaging Dustin's cheek with his hand.

"And you met him too?" Coldness in his voice, Amir eyed the squirmy Jordon, his face getting red with envy.

"Yeah, that's Al." Sounding snotty.

"I guess we're sticking with that then." Dustin smirked, As Jordon got a sneer from death.

"If we must." Flatly responding to Dustin.

"How about, just for the time being."

"Very well, for you." Death moved in kissing Dustin deeply.

"What the hell is going on?" Amir and to a lesser extent his side of the table were completely flustered by the happenings going on across from them. "Who is this guy?"

"He's a friend of the families." Dustin smiled, joyously.

"They met up at the pool party last night." Arman glowed, loving this, Gary and Amir were confused, and Jordon sat stewing.

"Pool party!?" Gary sat balking, mouth ajar.

"Yeah, there was a raging pool party after you two passed out. Until the cops showed up." Pausing as the server headed their way. "That was kind of a downer."

"I don't know, Jason got some good news." Dustin looked to put a positive spin on the sudden death to Arman's chagrin, making a sneer at Dustin for his snark.

"He got some bad news first!"

A very jealous Gary had to butt in. "Who's Jason!" His eyes going wide. Arman ate it up.

"The guy who died in the pool... So yeah, I see your point. That was I guess, bad news for him?" Addressing Arman, Dustin only gave Gary a cursory inclusion. "But he got good news after that. So that's a thing."

"Someone died in the pool?" Amir piped up, showing he had some measure of sympathy.

"Duh, that's why the cops showed up." Arman acted as aloof as Amir and Gary had the whole trip.

"Do you guys want a couple of minutes... Or another round?" Sharron moseyed up slowly. They'd seen the whiff of black streamers coming off the hot dude, yet were unsure if it was appropriate to approach, or for that matter, safe.

"I'd love another." Arman felt great, a tiny bit buzzed but not all messed up considering how much he'd already drank.

"Me too." Dustin seconded, then the guys. Jordon, peeping quietly, almost unassuming. Probably for fear of a berating.

"For you?" Looking at the stud with a certain familiarity.

"Perhaps a beer, or sweet mead? Perchance an ale?"

"When was the last time you had a beer? Like during the twentieth century or like before the inquisition?" Best to ask in these situations.

"I was there when Ninkasi tapped her vat. Does that count? And then briefly in Austria I had a few sips during the plague."

"So, it's been awhile. Beer's have changed some and the selection here is kind of limited, you may not like the current brands they have. You'd have to go to a microbrew for something you'd like. Same with the ale. Perhaps a distilled drink?"

"I suppose the wine selection isn't the best either..."

"Correct." Dustin and the figure of Mawt were unconcerned about the blank stares from opposite them, and Arman didn't count as he was able to handle the odd.

"Then yes, distilled. I'll let you choose."

"Let's do cosmos. A little sweet and full of booze."

"As you wish."

"The gentleman will do a cosmos also, please." Dustin was super chipper, it was a bit unnerving to Gary, Amir, and Jordon unaccustomed to him being outgoing.

"He's not really a gentleman though, is he?" Arman nudged Dustin's arm playfully.

"He's gentle, and in this form he's a man... Mostly. So he qualifies." Refusing to look over at Arman. Dustin bit Mawt's full pouty lip, nibbling for a very disrespectable amount of time while the server stood waiting.

"Okay, yeah sure..." Eyeing death, like they recognized him, however not able to place the face. Considering the face was an illusion, it wasn't any wonder.

"Please... You are Edger Bernstein's youngest, aren't you? Sharron, if I'm correct." Looking up at them, a slight smile on his full mouth recently paroled by Dustin.

"You knew my father?" Taken aback.

"I was with him in the hospice when he passed."

"Oh, so you worked there I guess, I thought you looked familiar." The pitch and twang in their voice coming through. "Were you one of his nurses?" That had to be where the server knew him from.

"Something like that. Edger was a very kind man. His only regret was that he didn't tell his children how proud he was of them more often when he was alive. Especially you, he was extraordinarily proud of you for standing strong to be the person you were meant to be." Looking directly at them, death's eyes reverted to the deep onyx pools, expressing the truth in his words. Sharron became misty-eyed and grinned, accepting this stranger's words as truth. Nodding, they left to get the drinks.

"That was sweet of you." Dustin reached over and gave the spectral creature a sensual smooch on the top of its curly-haired head.

In turn, it glared at Dustin with its own big puppy-dog eyes, full of lust and ravenous desire. "I am known to be very sweet." Wryly licking its lips for a serious make-out session.

"I know all about how sweet you can be..." Moving in for the hot and bothered.

"Nope: not at the dinner table!" Arman putting his proverbial foot down, and literally pulling Dustin back. Both Dustin and death whimpered softly.

"Someone died in the pool, and wasn't there someone at the bar too?" Amir was unsatisfied with the previous curtness about the night prior. "You told Gary something about someone in the bathroom!"

"Yeah, that's why we left... And if Gary didn't freak out, he wouldn't have broken his wrist!" Arman scowled at Gary, reaching for his fork to possibly stab Gary with.

"Sorry; I was high!" Anger slipping into Gary's voice. "It freaked me out that I got blow from a dead guy... Shit!"

Arman sneered, he was going to stab Gary, moving instead to his butter knife. It'd do some damage but unfortunately it wouldn't be lethal. Thankfully Mawt piped up, derailing the lot of them.

"If the sniveling mortal hadn't recklessly injured itself, Dustin would not have been there to help me with Addi? Who by the way, sends her regards and wishes you well." Speaking only to Dustin, his eyes glittering.

"You're right, thanks Gary." Smiling menacingly at the man, then back to the sexy apparition. "That was very sweet of her." Ever so slightly blushing.

"What had happened?" Arman tapped Dustin on the shoulder to get him to turn his attention away from his new beau for a few minutes at least. Before Dustin could answer the server returned with drinks, so an awkward conversation would have to wait.

"Anyone want to order?" Timidly asking, these guys were giving off some intense energy. Sharron could feel it like waves of heat. Pretty much the whole room could feel the tension rising, like a powder keg about to blow, and not in a good way.

"You know, I was wanting a tossed salad, but now I'm craving a Mediterranean platter... Care to share?" Looking lustfully at the dark-haired man, Dustin pursed his lips seductively.

"You make either of those sound so appetizing, how could I refuse." The spirit was so enwrapped, indeed Dustin was correct, he was at the mortal's mercy.

"K, since they're not talking about food, I'm going to steer this into a more PG-rated direction." Arman gagged at the smut talk, poking Dustin in the ribs.

Before losing his appetite he promptly ordered a big ass salad. The kind that middle America is known for. Meat, veg, more meat, eggs and a shit ton of fatty dressing. He could burn it off. Amir did his bacon cheeseburger, Gary wanted healthy so he got some lame ass turkey burger that wasn't healthy in the slightest. Cheese, grease and sodium, thinking he could work it off, Gary got yet another scowl from Arman and a strange sort of glare from Dustin's man. One that suggested "are you sure you want to do that" sort of warning look.

Jordon, acting as if he wasn't a complete loser spoke up quietly, not wanting to attract the ire of Amir or Al, as he called him. "What's the deal with the salmon?"

Sharron paused before answering, making a face that leads one to believe you're not going to like it. That pinched puckery lip, tilted head and lack of eye contact look. That kind of face.

"They had salmon last night, and it was on the buffet this morning. So the cook made a mouse. Honestly though, because of all that stuff last night, and the cops. Brad firing the lifeguard, and suspending some of the staff for, you know... What happened. I wouldn't recommend it." The phew face, and subtle nodding solidified it.

"What happened?" Gary acted genuinely curious. Amir and Jordon, perked up as well, they appeared to want to know, just didn't want to ask.

"Oh, I thought you knew. Brad said these guys pulled the body out of the water. I thought you were with them." Pointing to Arman and Dustin. There was some mild shock on the faces across from them.

"No, they were passed out, and that one..." Arman jabbed his finger at Jordon. "Did the walk of shame this morning." That would surely start another fight.

Whispering into Arman's ear, Dustin peeped "you're cold."

"I know, it's funny though." Arman peeped back.

"Oh! So do you want anything?" Realizing the longer they stood there, the more drama Sharron would have to be a part of, so best be direct. Jordon ordered a salad like Arman's. Sharron wrote it down and split. Possibly not to come back.

"So what the hell happened!" Waiting until the server left, Gary jumped. Completely ignoring that Arman and Dustin helped a person in any way.

"Epic sex party! A bunch of guys doing it in the pool house." Dustin wanted a turn at rattling the guys. It worked. "Arman jumped in to save the guy from drowning!" He made a snotty frown to Gary.

"Well, you helped pull him out." Casually addressing Dustin, while sipping his cocktail. "How did he die anyway?" Asking the one individual who would know for sure.

"A blood vessel in his brain ruptured, he went quickly." Replying as if someone had just paid him a compliment, and in a way Arman did. Taking an interest in his work, by his grin the spectre found it very flattering.

"Oh, hope it wasn't painful." Arman made a sad face.

"No not terribly. The person that was Jason Grant passed on very quickly, I hadn't even had a chance to kiss Dustin, it happened so fast." Smirking.

"He was passed out... That's a bit creepy, kissing him like he's sleeping beauty." Giving death a finger wag.

Dustin chuckled at Arman. "I was projecting, stepping outside myself. We were on the third-floor balcony at the time."

"As in..." Arman waved his hands about... "The spooky kind of projecting?"

"Yeah, wide awake outside my body."

"Hold up, so you're like a nurse or something? You knew the guy; the father... And you were at the pool?"

Amir had a rather puzzled look on his mug. He was very confused, skipping over this or that to handle the disconnections. Gary and Jordon were much more lost. All three were going to end up with painful headaches by the time the night ended.

"No, I'm not in the medical profession. However yes, I knew both of them and what happened." Smiling. Unsure if Dustin would want to tell them, or just make them suffer in their ignorance. The spirit would be fine with either.

"So yeah anyway... Who's Addi? Where'd you meet her?" Arman didn't need to recap with Amir, he'd been cut off from something he thought was actually interesting.

"A girl in the hospital, we saw her off." All pleasant and sweet sounding.

"Together?" A new facet to examine for Arman.

"He brought me over to the other side. It was touching, getting a chance to see her move on." Heartfelt from Dustin, and an only slightly eerie change in Arman's expression. Getting better at handling the weird only one eye and brow raised. Plus he'd kept his mouth closed this time.

"You can do that?"

"Oh yes, It's not often I have someone with me who understands the way of things as Dustin does." Molesting his face and head with his big meaty hands.

The PG rating was starting to go out the window again. Arman and the guys were pleased as punch the food began arriving so they wouldn't have to watch the obscene acts that would no doubt have taken place on the table if left unchecked.

Instead, they watched a whole different set of erotic foreplay. Dustin began feeding his friend, stuffing food onto his waiting and hungry mouth. Each bite was like a burst of excitement and wonder spreading across Mawt's face as he experienced new and intense sensations. The other's tried their best to eat, looking away as much as they could. However, it was very steamy with ample amounts of pent up sexual tension. Gary and Amir found themselves affected by the sight, Gary even appeared to be having some naughty thoughts about Dustin. Adjusting himself several times in his seat.

"Do they give you any ideas?" Using something that was perhaps supposed to be banter, Gary leaned across and whispered. "Like in a porno fantasy kind of way?"

"NO! Gary, gross... You're a pig! Stop rubbing yourself on the seat."

He'd been trying to eat and now his stomach flipped. The disgust of Gary's insinuation prevalent in Arman's voice. To sickening to watch anymore, Arman pelted Dustin the back of the head with a crouton to make them stop.

"Oh sorry..." He wasn't, but Dustin pulled his finger from the thick full lips of his companion who moved on to graze other things.

Breaking this awkward moment up, Amir put his hands up flustered. "I'm so confused! Look I know you think we're dumb..." Dustin cut in, having to make a correction.

"Amir, I don't think you're dumb at all. A bit of a whiner, and sometimes full of yourself; sure. But you're certainly not stupid in any way." Arman chuckled at Dustin for the brutal honesty.

Gary and Jordon got the cue. They weren't happy about it though, Jordon dropped his fork scowling. Gary pursed his lips tightly. If he wanted any shot with Arman, he'd stay quiet, but gauging from the shades of red he was turning, he would have liked to kick Dustin's ass.

Sure, there was a common belief, one that Dustin and Arman shared, that Gary was dumb. Also it was widely understood that for some reason Gary thought he was clever and smart, and often expressed betrayal at people when it was pointed out he wasn't. It was also often thought and openly discussed among all the guys that Gary acted like only one who was allowed to be a dick with impunity.

"Oh, um... Thank you?" Not sure how to take that. "I don't recall seeing him: you at the hospital." Figuring he should address the guy nibbling on a stuffed grape leaf next to Dustin. "But you saw him at the hospital and that pool party sex-capade thing?"

"Can I ask about this pool sex thing real quick?" Gary now bright red.

"I know where you're going with that; unlike you, we didn't do anything!" Waving his finger back and forth between himself and Dustin, the color on Arman's face offset the cherry red of Gary's. When Arman got angry his complexion took on a much more almond sepia tone, which was really quite fetching to most people. Angry Arman got many more complements on his deep brown eyes that happy go lucky Arman.

"I didn't do anything!" Adamant he raised his voice grabbing the attention of the few patrons in the place.

"You were feeling up those skank whores!" Arman's voice rose to match Gary's. Huffing, Gary piped down breathing heavily. "When we showed up, you were jerking that shit bag off!"

"Calm down Gary. We were hanging out in the corner. Pool party adjacent." Dustin shook his head, there was no reason for anyone to behave so angrily in public. Except Arman, who Dustin believed had every right to read Gary to filth in public, and would, in fact, encourage it.

This was a fun little sideshow, "Can we just tell them?" but it was tedious.

"Tell us what?" Amir asked quixotically.

"I don't mind." Turning to the reaper. "It's up to you."

"They are of little consequence to me, so if you wish to share, then I have no problem with your friends knowing." He nibbled a cucumber as he spoke, that bewitching voice and erotic manner Mawt ate was getting to Dustin and his tightening pants.

"After this trip, I'd say, calling them friends is stretching it *pretty far*." Making a sneer at the three across from him.

"Hey..." Jordon chimed in, sounding wounded. Like that the hottie viewed Jordon like the scum scraped off the bottom of a shoe, and that of all people, Dustin did as well.

"I guess we deserved that, but still." Amir raised his brow.

"Fine... Everyone stay calm... Nobody freak out!" Using the tone of influence, a feeling of ease washed across the room. "We've been calling him Al Mawt. From Arabic, it's loosely translated..." Not getting a chance to finish the why part.

"What do you mean calling him?" Amir queried.

"What's that mean... Al, whatever it was?" Gary looked around at Arman and Amir.

"How the hell should I know?" Amir scowled, getting cut off.

"He said it's Arabic, you're one of them."

"Gary you're an idiot, Amir's not Arabic." Dustin was getting a touch annoyed by these guys. *Honestly how stupid are they?* Asking himself. "Amir doesn't even speak Farsi!"

"How'd you know that?" A hint of respect in his tone perhaps.

"I pay attention."

"That's really cool." Nodding. Amir still had that growl like he wanted to punch Gary, no amount of charms would take that feeling away.

"Okay, whatever that is... So, what does mao-at stand for?" Flustered and visibly irritated, Gary's foot just went deeper, and deeper down his throat.

"It means death... I think?" Arman checked with Dustin. "It does right?"

"Yes."

"You don't know?" Again, Gary spoke out of turn. Managing only to position himself in the crosshairs for Arman to shoot him in the head.

"Why should I? I'm not great with languages, I only learned a few choice phrases in Punjabi growing up. Usually when my dad wanted me to take out the trash."

"I thought your dad was Indian?" That was the last straw. Gary was to be ignored.

"I hate you..." Arman seethed at him, turning back to Dustin.

"Sorry, but I don't know this stuff!" Not understanding the gist of a cold shoulder, he kept stumbling forward.

"That's just it though, you do. Gary, you've been to my parent's house for dinner. We've talked about my childhood, my upbringing... It's like my job, you were at the Christmas party last year, you met my boss!"

"Sorry, I don't remember..."

"Because you don't want to. It takes only a little bit of effort to pay attention to other people and you won't even do that!" Taking a deep breath. "Just stop talking. I can't do this with you anymore." Arman made a 'zip it' motion with his hand, done and done!

It was eerily quiet for several minutes, Gary had his head in his hands, trying to hold back some deep emotion that looked more like a hemorrhage to the folks at the table. Jordon, sliding his seat away from Gary slightly in case the guy exploded, worked up the courage to ask a question without getting his head ripped off.

XIV

"Don't anyone bite my head off… But why are you calling him death? If that's like what that is…" Jordon peeped.

"Well. He's got lots of names, Al Mawt, or death is just one way of saying it. Basically, it was for Arman's sake, so he'd stop calling him the grim reaper." Dustin smirked.

It would have been hard to imagine more confusion on the faces across from him, but there it was. The guys across from Dustin sat like corpses waiting for someone to reanimate their bodies for some soft shoe shuffling about.

"So, who is this guy then? Why would Arman call him the grim reaper?" Jordon, who'd been quiet, had the keen awareness to ask some pseudo-intelligent follow up questions.

"It's not so much about what we're calling him, as it is who he is. Arman had some questions when they met."

"Only a couple." Arman tried to play it cool. "Like why he was in the mirror then on the bed, but not at the same time."

"That's one question, another was the nature of what he is…"

Dustin felt it might go better to first sugar coat it for the guys, because they weren't the most open-minded, as their behavior demonstrated. Then if need be, he could slap them in the face with the skillet of reality. That would probably make their brains bleed so best to wait until there was no other recourse. That was his thinking anyway.

Unfortunately, the confusion was reaching a critical level where the bandage would have to be ripped off, and the wounds to their collective psyches would have to be lanced like a boil.

"I don't get it. So who is he, really? Some random guy you know, and why would you be so weird about it? Why call him death, that's dumb." Amir took a chance.

"What I was trying to say, it's not a name. It's who he is. Sort of. But not completely, it's more of an underlying principle..." Dustin didn't want to trivialize someone he wanted to bang.

"Let me try, cause you've been getting hung up on some weird ass, big picture shit." Arman stopped him. The guys would just get more lost than they had been. "He's death. The end of life! I've seen it."

"That's stupid." Gary blurted out. "He can't be, he's a guy, not a... Uh?"

"A corpse? I know right, but death isn't dead! Apparently..." Arman looked at the man next to Dustin stuffing his face with tabouli, simply smiling away. Gary perked up at not being berated by Arman.

"Huh?" Amir belched out. Jordon seconded the huh, with a "what?"

"Listen carefully. I know it sounds odd, but he..." Dustin put his hand on the guy's shoulder, caressing it. "Dude, save me some cucumbers." And of course, getting distracted by Mawt eating. He simply shook his head no, and chowed away, smiling.

"Dustin!"

Arman poked him in the rib to get his friend to focus, the lustfulness was just too much to watch. Being supremely disturbing to watch on so many levels, poor Arman had to have wished he knew where to get a fire hose at this hour to extinguish the four-alarm hormonal fire raging in Dustin's loins.

"Right; okay!" Making eyes at Arman. Stern, squinted eyes. "He, in this form, is human. However, he is, in actuality, a masculine embodiment of a destructive principle of one of the underlying forces of the universe. In this case the opposite of life, and one of the powers that be."

The combined look on Gary, Jordon and Amir's faces matched that of the wall behind them. Completely blank, with no clue as to what was going on or said. In its defense however, the wall had much more character. Deep shades of mahogany with a faux grain, making it look snappy. Dustin had to admire that wall, it was doing great, compared to the mammals across from him.

"Huh...?" After a minute or so Gary muttered.

"That's not what you said last night." Arman had a puzzled look.

"Well, you were a bit panicky."

"He leeched out of the mirror. And before that... You were hitting on him at the pool." He paused, momentarily rolling his eyes at the ceiling. "You know. You told me you wanted *him*, to ask *you* out. But if I recall, you made the first move at the pool, inviting him to come over, and then again in the room, and today. You invited him to dinner!" Arman proudly smiled at Dustin. "You really are becoming an extrovert, told you!"

"You're right." Dustin's eyes widened. He turned to death and smacked him on the arm. "What's that about?"

"I didn't know if you felt the same way." Bowing his head slightly and adding a sly grin.

"Oh horseshit. You dropped the ball." Tapping the human form hunk on his nose.

"Can we get back to where any of this makes any sense?" Someone had to ask, so since Gary and Jordon weren't, Amir did.

"Do you want to give it a go?" Dustin asked death, if only to keep him from eating the last cucumber slice, gripped firmly inbetween his fingers, ready to be devoured.

"I suppose I could. How to put it so these mortals understand?" Talking only to Dustin, Mawt receiving sneers from the guys.

"Go with your gut. Now that you have one." Poking the stud in the belly.

"Funny."

"What do you mean these mortals? You're insane." Gary was sounding a little bitchy. His ego was already bruised, he didn't appear to want any more trash talk about him.

"No, I am... Everywhere there is life, there is its opposite. Life is everywhere, so am I. I am the shroud, the great equalizer. The reprieve, the leveler." Taking a theatrical sort of pride, slightly twirling the vegetable around in his hand.

"Dude, you're on crack... This is stupid, Dustin, your date's crazy." Gary balked at the guy.

"Told you they wouldn't get the socio-political implications of that." Dustin stuck his tongue out at death. "Fine. His name isn't death. He is death... Happy?" There went the bandage.

"Um, hey guys, am I the only one noticing that the guy over there looks to be choking?"

Arman pointed to a single middle-aged white guy with a bad comb-over, at a table in the back, to the left of Amir's head. The other's looked, not overly concerned by the scene playing out. Most of the seven or so other people in the place stayed calm and didn't much respond either. It seemed no one was in a big rush to help.

"Yes, Jarrod Hewlett. He has some meat stuck in his esophagus." Death took a gander, smiled and went back to nibbling the last bits of food on his plate unphased.

This Hewlett person meanwhile, was losing control of his hair, while trying in vain to dislodge the slab of flesh in his throat. Slowly turning pink, his dyed blond hair flew up and sideways causing him to look a tad silly as his head bobbed back and forth. Much like a thanksgiving turkey running around without a head.

He was desperately gasping for breath at the same time desperate to swallow the hunk of slime slowly killing him. Sure he would be worried, just not terribly horrified that each passing second, the likelihood he'd die an excruciating death increased exponentially if aid wasn't rendered.

"If you are some death guy, shouldn't you do something?" Gary simply asked, as if it was just another facet of the conversation.

"That's not really what I do, however when he does perish, then I shall collect him." Still smiling.

"Why isn't anyone helping him?" Amir pondered aloud.

"Oh! That's my fault. I said *no one* freak out. Oopsy. I just meant you guys." Dustin who, now embarrassed, made a funny sort of grin cause he messed up. "Amir aren't you trained in first aid?"

"Yeah, and?" Not really making the connection, but he wasn't so much paying attention to Dustin speaking, as much as watching the guy and his hair flopping around.

His face was becoming many shades redder than a baboons butt. It looked funny, in a morbid comedy routine sort of way. Dustin, if he was a cruel heartless person could have sat and watched that all night, it would have much more entertaining than dinner with the buffoons at his table. He sighed, knowing something needed to be done before the guy croaked.

"Amir go help him." Dustin chirped, taking the high road was sometimes less interesting, however, it was supposedly more rewarding.

"Oh right..." Amir scrambled up, heading over to the man to perform the Heimlich. They were sure he'd succeed so Jordon and Gary turned their attention back to Dustin's companion.

"You don't know his name?" For once Gary didn't miss a beat, snapping back to the topic at hand. Probably because his features were contorted like his brain would seize up and stop any second. Like if he were a car, without any engine oil in it, kind of seizure.

"Gary don't be a dick!" Arman scolding the rudeness.

"Can you just show them?" Dustin made puppy eyes at the sexy male in the human meat suit.

Puckering his lips and batting his eyes, death, of course, would do it for his man.

"As you command, I obey." Softly and seductively responding. That made Dustin's heart skip a beat.

Watching the illusion fade from the sensual Adonis to the billowy smog covered shroud of a skeletal figure made Gary and Jordon's heart's also skip. However not in the same way.

The gauzy shroud was back trailing black vapors down and out across the floor of the room. The two tables of couples, the server and the bartender near the entrance, all backed away slowly as the form of this creature revealed itself. Somewhere between calm and afraid for their lives, Dustin's command of "no one freak out" was holding. However, all the folks in the room were far from comfortable with this current situation.

The middle-aged white guy who had food stuck in his breathing hole wasn't paying a lick of attention to the frightful scene, unlike the others in the restaurant. He had better things on his mind, like breathing deeply, filling his gasping lungs with air. Holding tightly to Amir's hand, he for some odd reason rubbed his forehead flesh to metacarpal flesh of Amir's. It must be one of those things middle-aged white guys do when their life is saved. Sure it was gross, but Amir still should appreciate the sentiment.

He thanked Amir profusely, very humbled by the experience, Jarrod Hewlett prayed to whatever it was middle-aged white guys pray to, whenever they have a near death experience. By doing this he was missing out on the experience of death nearby. All the whining and praying and greasy body parts were becoming a bit too much for Amir so he retrieved his hand after some effort, and wiped it on his pants.

The death nearby as it just so happened, was currently oozing cold blackness down and across the floor in their general direction, like long black steaming tendrils. Had he had the fortune to witness *this* spectacle, the middle-aged white guy might have learned a valuable lesson about chewing his food properly.

Sadly, this lesson would not be learned. So due to that one small thing, the person currently scaring the shit out of Gary and Jordon would be making a return visit to this very restaurant the following evening, because of a savory chicken entrée, and Amir would not be around to offer his hand to be used as a napkin.

Turning back to rub his smug self-righteous superiority in Gary's face because he did a good deed that Gary would never have bothered himself with, Amir's big beautiful jovial smile evaporated, gone in less than a second. Replaced with terror, the color fading out of him as he looked upon the bleak; black and slate blue shroud of death, with the gauzy mask covering its boney features.

"Allah Ackbar!" He shouted, pulling Arman's attention away from the spectacle back to Dustin. He'd seen the guy do this so he was less surprised.

"Isn't it Admiral Ackbar?"

"He's in shock." Nodding to Arman, then setting his sights on something completely different. "Yoinks... Now that you don't have a stomach, I'll be taking that." Snatching the cucumber slice out of the skeletal hand.

"Hey, that was the last one." Pouting behind his face wrapping.

"We can order more." Dustin nibbled it salaciously moving in to kiss the grim spectre of death.

"Gross... Stop doing that in front of me." Arman waved his hands in front of them. Watching Dustin make out was just a 'No'.

The shroud's appearance reverted back into the meat suit stud that was the illusion. "Is this better?" kissing Dustin deeply, and by the motion, sharing a bite of the cucumber in his mouth.

"No. It's weird and kind of gross watching Dustin make out with anyone. He's my best friend. It's wrong." Whining, he pulled Dusting back, breaking them up.

"What was that?" Amir slowly taking his seat. Sitting down was the best way to keep pissing himself.

"I think I pissed myself." Jordon gurgled hoping it wasn't a lot, alas he was definitely a little wet.

Unexpectedly Gary was handling the situation better than the others. He merely slugged his drink, then Amir's and hoped for more. He was ready to get obliterated. Holding the empty up he tried to get the server's attention. Sharron was watching but didn't really want to head over. Dustin solved that problem by silently motioning for another round for the table. His finger in a circling motion. The server nodded and headed to the bar. It would be the break from the strange they would need.

After what could best be described as an awkward pause, a few quiet moments with Gary's jaw open and dangling, words formed in his addled brain.

"Holy christ! I must be hallucinating?" Gary's spit hitting the table.

"Only if you're seeing the same hallucination as the rest of us." Amir sniped.

"It can't be, he can't be..."

"Gary, he's death. Face it, this is real, just accept that we all saw the same thing." Arman both annoyed and excited he had free range to run rough shot all over Gary for being an idiot was planning on taking to it like a junkie with a needle.

"So he's really death, like dead?" Reality slowly sinking into the overcooked meat of Gary's head.

"Apparently he's not dead, I know it's confusing."

Arman had the cutest expression, it was so evil looking. A long thin smile and gleaming eyes, his cheeks risen and brow dipped down in the center. It was so liberating, watching Jordon gulp, and Gary gawk, with Amir bug-eyed acting as if he might have a heart attack. Dustin wondered why he didn't scare the crap out of them long ago?

"In this form he's alive. As alive as anyone else, but in his real form, he's something else. The spirit of the moment of death." Dustin chewing as he spoke.

"K." Gary would need time to process.

Sharron returned with a tray of drinks, set them down stealth like, not speaking for fear of being drawn into what they could only believe was an elaborate practical joke.

"Can we get six shots, kamikazes." Dustin felt it would help ease the tension, or who knew, make things worse. But either way it would be fun.

"Absolutely, I could use six shots." Sharron just walked away.

Returning a short while later with shots, then away again back to the bar where Dustin watched the server and the bartender swig back three shots each. He chuckled quietly and focused back to the table. Downing the shots and ready to move on, except for some small thing he didn't prepare himself for.

The server without asking brought another giant tray of drinks and more shots to the table full of fresh cocktails and no empties. Each person at the small table had two additional rounds of drinks and shots before Dustin spoke. Realizing he messed up again, Dustin wanted to be cool and keep his faux pas on the down low.

"Were good on drinks, thank you." He whispered to Sharron.

This was only remotely odd in that, when Dustin made his circular motion earlier, he inadvertently enhanced his own "don't freak out" command. Clearly, he hadn't learned all he should have from his mother, who would remind him of that fact often. How she would know about this incident, well that was her secret and she wasn't ready to teach it to Dustin but he could hear her words in his head, *"that's what you get for holding out on us."* knowing full well there'd be a lecture when he got home. Her tune would probably change when she met his new lover.

All set on beverages the shroud continued. "I take the spark of energy, many cultures call a soul, and carry it on to where they will be taken to their destinations." The meat illusion attempted to explain for Gary. It was like talking to a potted plant.

Because Gary's brain left the building, Amir piped up. "What's that mean? What's the destination?"

"It depends on the energy. Some go back into the framework, other's move on to say, the land of reeds, the frozen lake. There's the womb of the mother, the great wood. It depends on who takes up the soul. Often it gets repurposed and sent back as another form." Death smiled at Amir.

"Framework? Who takes up these souls?" Amir still super confused but seemed to understand the concept better than Gary and Jordon, who both sat and stared.

See, Dustin thought, not dumb. Not smart but definitely not dumb.

"Again, it's dependent on which power claims them."

"Who are the powers, exactly?"

"The creative and destructive forces and everything inbetween, throughout all of creation. That reminds me..." Looking deeply into Dustin's eyes. "Hel is hosting a dinner party and has invited me. I was wondering if you'd like to accompany me." Big begging puppy eyes.

"That sounds interesting, what'll it be like?" Fascinated by the offer.

"Nemesis and Eris will be there for certain, they're bringing drinks. Some others including Anubis and Mommy-Ji are planning to come; I don't get invited often, so I'd be excited to go... If you are?" Timidly responding.

"I'd like that. It's a date."

"Be aware, the games can get a bit competitive unless Fortuna shows up. The party tends to die out quickly when she arrives; from what I'm told." Pulling back, not wanting to oversell it. Death would feel really bad if Dustin didn't like his friends.

"We'll stay away from gambling just to be on the safe side."

Hesitating slightly. "That reminds me. How would you feel about joining us? As one of the powers."

"Wait? Are you serious?" A very quizzical expression took hold of Dustin.

"Yes, I left earlier to discuss with the others. I don't often exert my will so they agreed easily." He looked so unassuming and wanting.

"What would I be doing?"

"Perhaps a sprite for starters. We'll start small see how you feel about it, and go from there?" Dustin raised a brow to this person's offer.

"Wait, so are you like offering him a job?" Arman chimed in. Busting with glee, the night just took a left turn into some new part of town.

"In a way, yes. It's not uncommon for the powers to include gifted beings. Most of the more well-known recruits are larger than life characters. What most societies call heroes. But really, there are many individuals who've joined, working behind the scenes as it were."

"Okay?"

"You still haven't explained these powers; it's just more vague confusion." Trying to catch up, Amir came off as snitty.

"They're what your people call gods... Is that better?" A pinch of irritation in his voice.

"Well, it's something. And you do what again? I'm just trying to understand..." Amir didn't need the attitude from the dead dude.

"He essentially takes the soul out at the moment something dies, and ships it over to the folks who'll process it..." Dustin liked that Amir was curious, and seeing as death was getting irritated, he'd take over for a second. "It's like when we checked in at the hospital. The receptionist found who we needed to check out Gary's arm, then we were sent to meet the X-ray tech. then the doctor. He's like the cosmic receptionist."

"That analogy's kind of weak. I get where you're going with it... But how about like, when we checked into the hotel. Brad was at the front desk and then he led us to the room." Arman liked his better, a lot cleaner. Dustin nodded approvingly.

"Except in his case when you check out... So, he'd be like what?"

"Concierge? Front desk attendant for the universe?" Arman spit-balled.

"The cosmic bell-hop!" Dustin exclaimed proudly. He and Arman were getting off topic.

"I don't like being a bell-hop. It trivializes what I do." Death sounded all pouty with Dustin. So, he just cupped the hunks face in his hands.

"Oh, sweetness. I know the work is important. I'm proud of what you do, and you should be too; my sexy bell-hop." Kissing the imitation face deeply.

"Stop it…" They were getting sickening again and Arman wasn't having it. "Back to the job! What's a sprite, and how is it people become whatever?"

"It's kind of like a cosmic bike messenger, sort of thing." Dustin made a squinting gaze at Arman, who he knew, would laugh. "Without a bike."

He did laugh, seeing right through Dustin's blustering. "A gopher… An errand boy for the universe. That's what it is. Am I right?" Waging his finger. "And how does someone go about applying?"

"It's much cooler than that." Dustin got a touch snotty. "Like a courier."

"Many mortals have gifts. The server, for example, has underdeveloped Psychic abilities. Mr. Davenport, if he could focus his energies and clear the blockages to his energy centers, could; over time, develop a mastery of bodily energy manipulation." Turning his sights on Gary, who was sneering. "Even Mr. Winslow has gifts. Atrophied and stunted, he could have the capacity for empathy. However, I don't believe he will ever develop his potential."

"Oh snap!" Arman burst out. Dustin, Amir, and Jordon chuckled loudly.

"Mr. Farahani has innate abilities that again, with energy work could be enhanced. Many mortal creatures are capable to become heroes as they're called. But few seldom do. In fact, many of the powers felt Dustin was too introverted to be useful. However, those of us who work in the background find his gifts useful."

Setting his sights on the big bad. "So, about that... Why exactly did you pick me? If the others think I'm not qualified?" A stern glare came over Dustin.

"I didn't... I never said you weren't qualified. Some of the powers felt you weren't outgoing. It wasn't me!" Dustin had death on the ropes, now pleading.

"Is it because of last night and us... Not because I am qualified? Or qualified, but not the first choice? Because why? Is it that you're only offering me a job, so we can date? Or is it, I have to date you for the job?" He gave death the third degree.

The poor deadly creature suddenly ambushed became shocked and a tad frightened by Dustin's interrogation. "What, no!" Standing up rapidly, he swooped, pulling Dustin up closely, intimately. "No. I like you... The offer's not dependent on that, nor that dependent on any offer. But yes, I want to spend time with you and this seemed like a good a way as any to do that." He exclaimed.

"Oh, sweetie. I was just worried." Taking his tone down a notch.

"No. I like you, being with you. I always have, I will continue to see you for all your life and be with you as long as you let me." A certain jealousy washed over Arman and the three stooges. In human form, this guy was the whole package and he was groveling at Dustin's feet. A collective *sigh* emanated across the table.

"Babe, I don't want a job I'm not qualified for, just to spend time with you. It wouldn't be fair, to you or the others." Caressing the face of his lover. "It doesn't mean we can't be together, I've waited for you too... perhaps too long. But now it's you and me, together." Pulling Mawt closer, resting forehead to forehead, the heat coming from them was electric.

"You worry too much. You're more than qualified, the job is yours if you want it. No strings, no conditions... And I'm going to stick close for personal reasons. That's non-negotiable." Death's lips edging closer. The guys could only sit back and watch.

"Just say it, you love me." Dustin begging him to be direct.

"Only if you love me..." Playful, with a tacky sort of snark.

"Well, I don't know?"

"Hey!" The faux pouty puppy face was too cute for Dustin to rebuke.

"Yes you idiot, I love you and have always loved you." Their lips met devouring each other for a few hot and bothersome minutes.

"So the job, is that a yes as well?" Nearly pleading.

"Definitely!" The quick pause from kissing to ask and answer, then back at it for a little bit longer this time.

"I've loved you for all of eternity." Whispering at Dustin while kissing him, death was rewarded by some steamy making out. Now all they needed was the background music to a porno and they'd be all set.

Across from them, Gary at least was getting a bit hard. He shouldn't have been, but being the lusty critter he was, never had much self-control over his penis. Probably why he and Arman had so many problems. Leering his pervy peepers over to Arman with the misplaced notion that Dustin's blooming love would somehow open Arman's blooming flower, Gary could see his now dead relationship had withered and shriveled like a centenarian's pucker hole.

Happy for Dustin, Arman didn't want to watch this heartfelt rom-com climax, so he busied himself sipping his cocktail, checking out staring faces of the bystanders in the restaurant. They were hostages to all this life, death, and worst of all; love playing out like bad dinner theater. Cheesy shtick while they were trying to eat. Just as the dripping tugs of the heart reached its creepy crescendo Arman caught sight of Gary glaring at him.

The sad desperation in his eyes, hoping the corpse of their failed life together could be resurrected. If anything, Arman would attach some heavy rocks and sink the body of their love deeper into Gary's lake of despair. He met the sad leering face of the man he once called lover, with cold stone. Finishing one drink, then moving on to the next. Leaving the empty discarded and unwanted, like Gary did to Arman's feelings. After the last forty-eight hours, Arman was surprisingly okay with letting Gary drift away down the rapids.

Much longer than most would argue was an undue length of time getting acquainted with the inside of each other's mouths, Dustin and his deathly lover came up some much-needed air. Not air for them, but a breather from the realization this guy wasn't like any other guy anyone in the room had met. So Dustin's traveling companions would need time to consume it all. They'd have time for that, just not for a little while longer.

"Can I borrow your phone again?" Dustin batted his lashes at Arman.

"Um yeah..." Happy to oblige now they stopped sucking face.

As Arman began to pass his phone over, he felt the buzz as it came to life. A call was coming through, it hadn't rang yet, but the display lighted up. Clearly wanting no part of that one he rapidly passed it off.

"Hey Marta, change of plans..." Dustin clicked the phone to answer and spoke as if his mom was just on the other side of the table. "We'll be swinging by tonight, and meet the guys tomorrow back on the road." A short pause as if she expected this. "Yup, I'm bringing someone."

Some giddy chatter on the other end as Dustin leaned over to his beau. "Where's Hester?" He whispered.

Softly replying, "Her connecting flight has just left O'Hare." His satin voice whispering into Dustin's ear.

Mouthing a thank you, Dustin, returned to the chat. Now that the people on the other end shut up long enough for him to have an opening.

"No way... I'm not telling you who, that's a surprise." He made a long scowl. His mom was taxing. "I'll tell you this much, he's an old friend of the family." More chatting, they were abuzz on the other end. "We'll be there by the time Hester pulls up."

Arman had a growing list of questions, meanwhile, Gary for whatever reason was becoming more agitated. Jordon and Amir watched, this scene was too strange not to.

Death sat back down contentedly nibbling little bits of vegetables and sipping his beverage. Dustin was trying hard to get a word in, waiting to pounce, attempting it and being shut down. He was outnumbered on the other end and getting annoyed. Wishing he never answered, except he'd need to prepare them, and by extension, his grandmother who would be walking into a hurricane of madness. Barking shrieks and howls of folks in the background were coming through loud and clear, Dustin waiting to speak kept pulling the phone away so his eardrum wouldn't rupture.

No wonder Dustin had been jealous of Arman's home life, there folks were given a modicum of privacy. By the voices, it seemed the collective hive was swarming over the news their boy was bringing a date. He slumped back into his chair shaking his head.

"Yeah... So we'll be there then, you can meet him when we get there!" Snapping. "Mom I don't know what the regional food is here..." A change of subject. "No, we haven't had dessert either," cut off again. "Pie? Fine. I'll stop and get a pie."

Squinting over to look at the shroud of death in stud form Dustin whispered again. "Can we make a stop on the way? They want pie." His attention was drawn back to the call as many audible voices cried out at once.

"Anything you like." Puckering his thick lips at Dustin. Death just super thankful he wasn't on the call.

Nodding, his attention was dragged back into this stupidity. "I have no idea where to get a sloe-berry pie at this hour..." Another pause.

"No... No, loganberry either, we'll stop at a market on the way." His idea wasn't well received. Thinking *do it your damned selves then!* Dustin kept his calm. "I'll grab a blackberry... Who cares?"

Apparently, the folks on the other end of the phone stopped worrying about who Dustin was bringing home, instead, turning their collective focus on what errands they could have him do on his way. This was becoming much too irritating for Dustin, absurd for Jordon and Amir. It was hysterical for Arman and death was all content like. Gary reached a breaking point, however. With a soft "excuse me" he quickly rose from the table and huffed away.

Gary would no doubt expect someone to rush to his side. Probably Arman and that wasn't going to happen, nor did it appear, anyone else felt like it either. Only cursory glances to Gary's backside were made as he paced out of the room. Even Dustin had to admit; in jeans, Gary had a great ass. He thought he was an ass, and never wanted to touch Gary's ass, but if he were a stranger off in the distance, he'd comment on that ass jealously.

"Is he coming with us then?" Now was as good a time as any to enjoy his salad, so Arman ate while the odd was happening.

"He has too. His wallet and keys are in his bag, and that's locked in the car." Jordon said flatly.

"He's such a dick." Amir adding as he bit into his now cold meal.

"Marlow still has the market, right?" Back at it with his family. "We'll stop there." Another short pause as Dustin chortled. "You call him..." His eyes widened, exasperated. *He was doing them a favor* and now regretted it. "Because I don't want too... Make Marlow do it, or I'll tell Amanda how he really injured his back." That shut his dad up at least. Some of the voices on the other end burst into laughter. "Yes mom, I know how it happened, we'll be home by the time Hester gets there... Love you too." Dustin hung up the call. "They're so annoying!" He barked at the rafters.

"I got to tell ya, I don't remember your family being so... What's the word?" Arman smirked at Dustin.

"Batshit? Sugar-crazed lunatics? Because that's what they are... Hester's date ends poorly, so because of that and meeting him, my family wants to do the whole late night gabfest." He rolled his eyes.

"Sorry." Arman tried to hold back his gleeful smile.

"You're so lucky to have emotionally distant parents." Scowling.

"Rude!" He pelted Dustin with a crouton. The floor was going to need a good sweeping after these guys left.

"It was a compliment... Jerkface." Sticking his tongue out playfully.

"Um-hum... You know, I have a couple of twenty or so questions, if you don't mind?" Arman glowered smugly at Dustin.

"Wait. I can't even understand, what anything just happened, are you really getting all this?" Jordon made the attempt to ask a straightforward question, unfortunately, the situation had so many bendy curves that it would be nearly impossible not to get lost. Within a bigger context, of the bigger context.

"Huh?" Pausing for a hot second. "I mean most of it, to some extent sure... But Dustin, really just a couple of questions." Arman wasn't going to let Jordon distract him.

"Yeah shoot."

"Do you know why Gary stormed off?" The first thing that popped into his mind.

"Not a clue..." Smirking.

"He's not going to try and take off is he?" The thought of leaving Gary was appealing but could be considered a dick move and that was more Gary's style.

Death took this one. "The sulking mortal is leaning against your vehicle. By his vitals, he is agitated and upset." So contented and chipper.

"Cool. I suppose that means we'll have to take him with us." Arman seemed almost disappointed.

"You could drop his ass at the airport. Or better yet, leave him here." Dustin offered options.

"No, the people here have been through enough already. We'll take him. Maybe he'll grovel the whole time?" About the most sympathy Arman could offer.

Jordon had some concerns, and thought now would be a good time to ask. "So, you can see Gary? Like now, out by the car." Dustin pictured the hamster wheel turning in Jordon's head.

"Yes."

"How?"

"Jordon, he's death. Everywhere." Amir got it, putting a sympathetic hand on his partner's shoulder.

"So, you know what happened last night? With me?" Becoming embarrassed.

"Yes." Death had a sort of look about him, one that suggested mild disgust.

"Ugh." Jordon turned beet red at this point. Amir removed his hand scowling. He'd have some questions later.

Not wanting to ponder Jordon being a skank, Arman shifted gears to happier things. "And how exactly are you guys getting to Santa Fe? And wherever your cousin, or uncle whoever is at?"

"Marlow. He's Nate's brother. He's in Albuquerque. So we'll pop by there grab some food then pop over to my parent's house. I'll catch up with you guys tomorrow."

"Where?"

"Wherever you're at, we can meet you there."

"How?"

"It's super easy." Using his big buff lover as a prop. Dustin placed his hand over the handsome illusion's hand. "Think of it this way. My hand on his like so..." As he spoke Dustin moved his hand up to death's shoulder. "The shoulder is the destination. Just like that, we move from place to place."

"That make's no sense..."

"Sure it does."

"I am in all places, anywhere there is life there is me. My form encompasses all reality."

"That's disturbing..." Amir peeped, one angry eye still on Jordon.

"It is! But, does that mean you what? Teleport. Go from here to there by some... what?" Arman was keeping the focus on this, any petty and really creepy implications for Jordon could wait.

"Well, no. Teleporting is like with the Heisenberg uncertainty principle and all the odds and probabilities of trying to go from place to place and knowing where a particle will be... This is more like spooky action at a distance!" Dustin believed he was clear, even making a bit of a joke as a way to keep it light.

"Huh?" It didn't work, Arman was as blank-faced as the rest.

"Yeah, like teleportation." His face went flat.

"Cool..."

"And on that note, we should head out. That is if you'd still like to meet with the others?" The figure of death breaking up the awkward pause. Dustin didn't know how to explain any clearer, and Arman didn't know how to understand it any differently so they were just sort of quiet.

"I suppose we should. Hey, do you think I'll get horns?" good time for a subject change he thought.

"If you'd like. Or you could try on some different faces and see which one you prefer." Options from death.

"Faces?" Jordon gurgled, a little drool coming out.

Too much more of this and Dustin would have to check Jordon in somewhere. He was feeling and processing things his brain had no framework for. Troubling and new things. It would take time, if ever for him to process, but at least as far as Dustin was concerned, he could be put in some kind of padded cell away from any harm to himself or others. Plus, the guy Jordon had been super hot for, was not the guy he thought he was. Add to that, seeing him as a phantasm made the hard-on go bye, bye.

Now, to know that this guy could spy on him anywhere? That was giving Jordon a new kind of twitching in his butthole. A kinky and disturbing kind of twitch. For the first time in his life, his mind, not his cock, was being blown. And unlike every blow job he'd gotten, this was epic.

"Not actual faces! I'd be trying on new looks." Dustin glared.

"Why, your face is already scary enough." Arman playfully jabbed.

"HA, HA, HA. Funny." Deadpan. "So do we need to hug it out, or are we good?" Smirking.

"Hug the big bad, we're good. You kids have fun, and play nice with the other ghouls." A broad smile spread across Arman's face.

"You still have the card? Spend whatever you need, Marta will find a way to cover it." Dustin double checking, he was stoked but didn't want to leave Arman in a lurch.

"It's fine, I've got this: GO!" Shooing Dustin off.

"Cool, we'll pop in on you guys in the morning." He and the big bad got up to leave as it were. "If you need anything just ask for Al." Dustin beamed at his lover.

"Funny." Who didn't look amused.

"I sure will. And um, a couple of quick things... I'm going to ask you later how your mom's going to cover this. Because I'll be leaving an obscene tip for the server." Wagging his finger.

"You better, imagine if this happened to us." Dustin grinned.

"And, don't drop in while we're driving. I'd rather not meet you on the other side... If you know what I mean." More finger-wagging.

"I do, and I won't. We'll wait till you stop to eat." Smirking.

"And just one more, small, miniscule, unimportant little thing..." Getting a look from Dustin, that 'go on spill' kind of big-eyed look. "Why did we get the impression your family wasn't shocked or surprised in any way, that you're showing up tonight... There's a shit ton more, but I'll leave it with that." Pandora had her box spread wide open already. Arman didn't need to route around in there any more than he had.

"He's not the first friend of the family I've brought home." Dustin being all like 'duh' as his taste in men was known to be odd.

"Ah ha! I knew it! Who was it? Bennet I bet..." Arman excitably stood and jabbed his finger at Dustin cheering.

"No!" Dustin became adamant.

"Bull! He was a total freak!" Arman, equally adamant.

"Who's Bennet?" Amir leaned in to ask.

"This scary ass dude, Dustin dated freshman year of college. Like a satanic goth biker guy. Head to toe in tattoos, beefy, muscular; dressed in leather. Loved to play with knives. He always claimed he was a vampire." Arman was giddy to share.

"Did I ever meet him?" Amir had met several of Dustin's lovers. Most of the time he never really paid much attention to Dustin, let alone his boyfriends.

"No, not him..." Turning back to Dustin. "He *was* a vampire or something right?"

"No! Granted he was hot... And he did like to drink blood, but he was completely normal." Dustin got a tiny bit flustered at his relationship choices being called out.

"Eh, on so many levels. So, is that why you guys broke up? He wasn't the undead hottie of your dreams?" This new knowledge about Dustin opened a whole avenue of teasing for Arman. It would be like heaven, which he'd have to ask about later.

"The reason I dumped him was he was a dead lay. Just laid there. If I wanted to be that bored, I would have studied." Dustin narrowed his eyes at Arman.

"Ewww... So who then?"

"You remember that guy Belarus. Hester set me up with him to get to know his grandmother; she's a baba yaga. He and I are still friends, but lovers... No."

"Good." A ring of envy in deaths sultry voice.

"Ah, honey, no reason to be jealous." Moving in for the smooches. "Belarus was cute, but he was kind of dumb."

"Ah-hmm! Then who?" Interrupting.

"If you can believe it. Ken."

"Ken Tenaka? That Ken? He was so normal. Like painfully normal... Which for you was weird, but he wasn't a monster or anything!" Shocked and amazed at this new insight.

"Thanks?"

"Bitch, you know what I mean. Ken Tenaka's ambition in life was to become an acquisitions manager at a brokerage firm!" Arman turned to Amir still trying to follow the odd. "You met Ken."

"I did?" Amir's face was blank.

"You did. Several times. We dated for a year but I never expected you to remember him. Half the time you acted like I wasn't around." Dustin spoke nonchalantly.

"Wow, I deserved that. Have I mentioned I'm sorry about that? I am." Amir looked squarely at Dustin; his apology was sincere this time.

"I wouldn't mind hearing it more often, but thanks." Nodding. "But we're not going to hug it out or anything, just so you know." Waving his hand about at Amir. He nodded.

"So anyway bitches, Ken?" Focusing back on to something interesting. "How was he in any way, a friend of *your* family?" Proverbially speaking, Arman genuinely wanted to know.

"Ken was possessed by an Ikiryo. So, it was like dating two guys at the same time. I thought it was nice. One guy who was super sweet, the other super adventurous." Dustin's eyes sparkled with an evil gleam. "Too bad they moved to California." Reminiscing with a smirk that was a tad bit too wide for death's liking.

"Hey..." Bumping shoulders to draw Dustin back.

"Again, you have nothing to be jealous about." Showing his big soft eyes up at his man, thing.

"And again, focus..." Arman butting in, before anyone got the butt in public. "You're a freak, we'll chat more when I see you...Because once again, I have no idea what anything you said, means. Now skedaddle!" Suspecting they'd stop somewhere and do it. There was to much sexual tension between those two for them not to.

"Fine, but wherever you guys stop, better have waffles!" Dustin backed away with a big broad smile.

Arman had such a light-hearted feeling he didn't know if he should laugh or be in awe as Dustin and the specter slowly misted away into a billowing black cloud. As the fog evaporated, so did they, gone.

For a short while, Jordon and Amir sat quietly, blankly staring at the open space where Dustin and the hunky dude were moments before. They had been trying to make some sense of any of this and would need time. The other folks in the place weren't certain if everything that happened was an elaborate show or not. The server however, didn't much care and hastily dropped the check. The table might not be finished but Sharron was. They'd wait for Arman and the other two out until they left.

Because so much time had passed and no one came out to sooth Gary's bruised ego, he moseyed back in, slowly sitting. Cantankerously glaring at the others. Jordon and Amir weren't reacting to much of anything, just drinking. Arman gave Gary an unphased eye roll and went back to his meal, almost finished.

"Where'd Dustin and what's his face go?"

Gary should have realized he was stunted, and in need of the help Dustin asked his dad for. There was no way Dustin wanted to be trapped with his dad's men's group purging repressed emotions pushed deeply down. Gary, on the other hand, would benefit greatly if he partook. He wouldn't, as his expression gave away. Desperation and desire that was borderline stalkerish had taken ahold of Gary's features. Arman was his obsession. So sad, and as Arman watched him, made the connection to just how sick Gary was.

Without a swift smack upside the head, Gary may slide off the deep end and do something desperately foolish. Like stand under a window and serenade Arman. Or leave a person-sized apology cookie at Arman's work... That should give anyone shiver's.

"They left. We'll meet them tomorrow for breakfast." Smiling his big fake ass smile.

"Oh, okay." Gary thankful he had several full drinks, and that there were ample leftover drinks untouched by anyone else. He'd help out and make sure none went to waste.

XV

Surviving the week, at the tail end of the weekend, Arman sat at a quaint little repurposed wooden table, in a folksy little café some two blocks away from Marta's shop. Now, this calm Thursday morning, the café had just opened as the new days light whipped up the winds, a fresh breeze wafted through the wide space. Waiting for Dustin to arrive, Arman was content to sip his latte in the calm tranquility of the space watching the swirl and bustling of the foot traffic on the street. Across from him, Jordon and Amir were chilling out at a separate table by the back.

Jordon sat legs crossed attempting to meditate on the pillow covered bench by the window. Amir slouched back in his chair grooving on the world music playing over the sound system. Arman hadn't fully adjusted to how much these guys had changed and hoped to discuss it with Dustin when he showed up. That and a few other things, like how Dustin's mother kept Arman up all hours of the night, prattling on about this and that.

In her defense for the late nights, Marta Ney did give him use of a private space, a lucrative job offer, and ample weed. So, he should be able to bite his tongue for a short while at least.

Jordon looked so much different than he had the entire trip, not only was he focused on his breathing, hands on his knees; he was wearing loose-fitting yoga pants, sandals, and a white blousy shirt. Steeped perhaps too much in the suburban Zen trope, his face now sported a scruffy beard thing. The kind of unattended hair, that the one weird teenager tries to grow to show his friends he's hit puberty. Spotty here and there, it was by no means a full beard, just patches of pale blond facial moss.

Amir to his credit made the 'letting it all go' look work. His beard, also unkempt was filling out nicely adding authenticity to his features. There was no product on his black mop top so he had some bounce. His yoga pants were baby blue to go with the hippy shirt, and (thankfully) he wore slip-on beach shoes to hide his gangly toes.

Eyes closed, he sat drifting off as if he was stoned out of his mind. He may well have been, he and Jordon were trapped for three days and nights, prisoners of Nate's men's group. Learning energy work, sexual healing and many other frightening things males do behind closed doors when they wish to detox their souls.

Arman's friends went on many peyote and mescaline fueled spirit quests, pot-infused edible vacations, and many, many magic mushroom adventures. This morning was their first day away from the yurt and the twenty odd males lurking inside.

Like really odd, well-meaning liberal weirdo's, trying to debunk patriarchy by crystal healing and reiki. Arman so pleased he wasn't inducted into the circle, he had better things to do. One of which he'd tell Dustin, now materializing outside of the café. His boyfriend, always around wasn't visible so Arman took it as a sign he had to work.

"Morning." Chipper and bouncy, the glittery ethereal dust sparkling off his frame and disappearing back into nothing. This new Dustin was something, and would take a little time to get used to.

"You're in a good mood." Arman trying to shake off sleepiness.

"It's been a good day so far, how're things around here?" Smiling so brightly, the freshly fucked look was a tad too much to handle at this hour.

"Gary left before stepping foot in the house and your mom's been driving me up a wall... And then there's these guys. Morning!" Toasting Dustin with his extra large latte.

Dustin made a humorous scowl then excusing himself, he headed directly to the counter to order caffeine for them both. This was about to get dishy, and Dustin needed his friend to be awake yet maintain his slightly bitchy attitude to squirt out all the good gossip, like only a ripe fruit can.

"So where to start?" Back at the table, Dustin sat, pondering the juicy choices.

"Let's start when you bailed after we got here. Leaving me alone with your parents and them." Motioning to Jordon, looking more constipated than meditative.

Arman had the bitchy part down, so Dustin figured best to try a new track. "Sorry about that, I was excited to start learning all the tricks of the trade." Making a broad, shit eating grin.

"Um-hum. And how's that going?"

"Pretty good, for the most part. I can materialize on the spot. But I'm having trouble holding things while I travel." Dustin spoke as if Arman had any clue of what that meant.

"K?"

"I mean, when I go all misty, I have some issues with carrying stuff, my clothes and wallet and stuff, sure. But like documents, letters, and heavier objects... I've been dropping them." By the faces Arman made, Dustin was a bit clearer.

"So, no moving furniture then?"

"No... Not yet." Flipping Arman off.

"Perhaps it's you getting distracted. I bet the men's group could help you focus. Like the way, your dad helped those two." Arman again motioned, this time to Amir, eyes closed jamming out to the sounds of a didgeridoo.

"Yeah no. What's up with them anyway?" Dustin looked concerned. Wondering if they were broken?

"I was going to ask you the same thing."

"I can try."

Sighing, because Dustin didn't really want to see Amir or Jordon the same altered way he could see life and death in waveform. The spectral vision radiating their auras like radioactive residue. To Dustin, it would be like if any normal person, watched one of those horrendously disgusting cosmetic surgery shows about liposuction.

The ones, where all the fat and blood ooze all over, and the patient is jostled and tossed about the table by the tube stabbing and sucking its way to a sexier, more youthful appearance.

He believed it would look something like that. Dustin was much more relieved when he got over his anxiety and glared. Their chakras or energy centers, were nearly aligned and almost opened fully. That was shocking in itself, like the two men had some form of spiritual high colonic. In hindsight, Dustin grossed himself out more by thinking about the cosmic enema bag that routed around inside them, than what he actually witnessed.

"Anything?" Arman intently watched the strain on Dustin's face, like watching someone try to piss in front of a cheering crowd.

"Kind of..."

"What; is he going to burst from some sort of intergalactic puss exploding from a pimple?"

Dustin stared at Arman with a disgusted gaze. "Gross! No. And stay out of the library at the house, that room is the stuff of nightmares." Referring to his parent's study.

"Tell your mom to stop dragging me in there. That's the strangest room I've ever seen."

"You haven't been in the attic yet." Dustin puckered his lips like he swallowed a box of lemons. "One disturbing thing at a time." Trying to focus back on the hippy jock hybrid.

"Sorry." He wasn't.

Dustin scowled. His weak attempt to be mad. Letting his eyes shift completely to the other place, Dustin could focus, now that Arman piped down.

"He's sort of half outside himself. Jordon's attempting to project his spirit, he's got a kind of connecting umbilical cord attached to his head. Frankly, I'm surprised he's made it that far. He should be proud." Dustin's head tilted seeing Jordon this way. It was different and not something even he could have foreseen just a week before.

"I'll be sure to tell him you said that." Smirking.

"Oh, you're a bitch. Honestly, it hasn't been that bad around here, has it?"

"No, just a lot of change really quickly. These guys went into the yurt, and now we have this. It's like their pod people."

"In a way, they've always been tools. Now they're useful tools?" Shrugging empathetically.

"Lame..." Arman scoffed at his bad humor. "I can't quite get used to them like this. They're talking about heading to Sedona to an Ashram or some shit... It's weird." Arman glared at Amir staring up at the ceiling, focused on one point. A water stain, and a small one at that; held his entire attention span. "It's like they joined a cult."

"In a way they did. They got stuck in the yurt with my dad. He gets in people's heads. He means well but..."

"I liked them better when they were selfish, now they're like zombies."

"It will get worse if they stay. They're losing their ambition. I'll drop them back tomorrow, so they get a swift kick in the ass from the real world." Eyeing Jordon up and down, his astral form looked like a breach birth only halfway out and sideways. It was kind of disgusting.

"So when you say you'll drop them off, you mean the big bad, because if you do it they'll what? Slip through your fingers? Only some of them will end up at home and the rest will bleed out like... A big spongy pile of goo?" Eyeing Dustin suspiciously.

"That's cruel. True, but mean. My way sounds so much more elegant." Dustin made a wide toothy grin.

"Speaking of, where is he?" Ignoring Dustin, Arman started on the second latte.

"You my friend, are a bitch this morning." Sticking out his tongue. Arman chuckled. "He's around. Right now, he's hanging by the pastries."

Dustin nodded over to the glass counter, like the tables, it too was repurposed. The long bulky glass and metal frame were from an old cafeteria counter. They maybe should have the refrigeration checked, because Mawt materialized his black and blue gauze covered hand above the scones. Waving his skeletal digits at Arman in a playful motion. Arman tipped his cup back at the hand and continued to sip.

"Sup..." To the spirit of death collecting expiring bacteria. "So, I guess we should shy away from the treats?"

"Probably best." Dustin smirked.

"If you drop kick them back to Scranton, will they survive, now that they're like this?"

"They thrive in reality. It'll take some time, but they'll be better for it. If they stay here, they'll just become two more, lazy hippy slugs Marta adopts."

"Like children?"

"No, you're adopted like a child, they're more like pets. Mom lets them hang around until she realizes they're not house trained, then sends them back to the real world." Dustin spoke casually about it.

"I've met enough of those this week." Suddenly getting animated. "That reminds me, your old boyfriend Sunbow is back!"

Arman jabbed his finger in Dustin's face. Dustin went from an empathetic concern for Jordon and Amir to a rather horrified stare at Arman.

"Marta didn't tell him I'm here! Did she?" Dustin's outline began to fray, trembling like a glitter fountain. He was going to make a break for it, evaporating into the ether leaving pixie dandruff in his wake.

"Cheater." Arman barked.

Now that Dustin was something in between a man and a spirit, he had this wonderful ability to materialize and dissipate anytime he wanted. It saved a butt load of time and money on travel, however, he could now slip away unnoticed leaving Arman in awkward situations without a wingman. In the past, Dustin used his innate abilities to stand unseen and unnoticed quietly in the background.

Listening and watching people do all sorts of things, things people only do when they don't think anyone's watching. Arman knew this about Dustin and often utilized it to his advantage. It was always great there was someone hiding in plain sight Arman could go to, when groups became too much. Not to mention getting the scoop on everything about everyone.

Now Dustin had this extra ability that made situations questionable. If Dustin got bored or worse, caught in a room with say, Jordon doing unspeakable things to a stranger for money, Dustin could immediately disappear. Instead of his normal plotting a way to the nearest exit, generally running into other people doing unspeakable things along the way. His new gifts were a great benefit for his sake. It saved Dustin a lot of time and drama. It didn't help Arman so much.

Now Arman would be caught without a heads up, and already on this trip, he'd stumbled into situations where it would have been really helpful to have his eyes seared out. All because Dustin fled. Arman wanted some ground rules. A signal flare perhaps? Anything that warned Arman not to go into the kitchen at Dustin's parent's house during meal times. Unless of course, he wanted to see Nate and Marta rekindle their relationship over the main course.

The extended family ate a ton of take-out most evenings. Arman was later warned by Hester, Dustin's grandmother that large festivals and events brought out the lascivious side to the couple. They fed off the sexual energy or something like that.

Just one more thing Arman now knew, and deeply regretted knowing. Being adopted into this clan as an honorary member of the Ney family, meant he was learning what those childhood monsters that hid under the bed were hiding from.

"No, I told him you already had a boyfriend, and he was the jealous type." Arman smirked.

"Thank you... Speaking of the jealous type, how'd it end with Gary?"

"I never told you we ended it, I just said he left." Dustin spoiling the ending again and happy about it.

"Same difference."

"We barely spoke on the way to the airport, he's looking for apartments back home. Said he'll be gone by the time I get back." Arman had mixed feelings. He wasn't that upset. He was almost upset at not being more upset.

"Wow, that's good I suppose. Have you told anyone yet?"

"My parents. They were ecstatic. Mom wants to set me up with a guy from her church. I told her it was too soon." Sipping his latte.

"Ouch. I almost feel bad for Gary, I don't, cause he's a prick, but almost." Dustin shrugged, this wasn't a celebratory or a mourning event, just inevitable.

"I have to give him some credit. He finally admitted he cheated on me. On four separate occasions, so yeah... That's when any chance of us staying together died." Arman had that look of remorse in his eye. Too much time wasted on his ex.

"I'm sorry. You always knew he did, at least he admitted it... If it helps, I can tell you what's going to happen to him after he dies." Dustin wanted to put a positive spin on the situation for Arman. "It's bad! Well for him..." He made a big surprised face, eyebrows flailing up and down for comic relief.

"A dog?"

"Worse..."

"Oh wow, save that for my birthday. I already have something to cheer me up." Matching with his own comic brow motion.

"Do tell!"

"Your mom offered me a job. Doing the online sales and distribution." Smiling slightly.

"I thought you were going to complain about her?" A bit puzzled, this was news.

"Oh, I am... But this is the good part of the story. I'm thinking of moving, now that Gary's not tying me down. And you can show up whenever you want and your mom offered me the job... And the apartment, plus help with moving." Arman cracked a smile. "It'd be a nice break from Scranton."

"That's great... I think, and you're okay with all the crazy of the family?" Dustin was happy for Arman, however, concerned because of what Arman would be walking into. "This *is* ground zero for the alien invasion, so you'll be in the bullseye if you move here." Not wanting to dissuade Arman, as much as warn him.

"Yeah, since you bailed, I've gotten a crash course in the Ney family traditions. While those guys were getting their chakras aligned on the astral plane, I've been stuck in family meetings until sunrise every day."

"By the gods." The shock on Dustin's face. "That was quick... Robert's Rules, or parliamentary procedure?"

"Consensus." Arman was stern in his reply, noting the severity of the events.

"Those monsters!" Dustin's face reflected his disgust over the rampant bureaucracy implicit in his family. "Why? Aside from the farce of Marta's tax write off, what scheme were they hatching?" He referred to the supposed 'interfaith conference' his mom was allegedly hosted that week. It was merely a ruse to drum up tourism dollars for the family's businesses.

"Nothing so diabolical, wingnut." Arman chuckled. "It started out with your mom complaining that you could have easily run an errand for the shop."

"Was that the note on the fridge Sunday morning? Marta wanted me to stop and get something? Why wouldn't she just ask..." Breathing to calm himself, such drama.

"She was upset because you wouldn't go pick up the crystal idols for her." Arman tried to keep a straight face.

"I can't just pop by Tibet anytime she wants some hand carved crap, just to save a few dollars on shipping!" Dustin rubbed his eyes in frustration.

"I know, and she posed the question that, 'with your new found gifts' you should be able to help the family more." Thankful he didn't have to deal with this directly. Arman was now an active participant, just not the target.

"One, I never read that note, I was in a hurry. And two, I'm not my mom's gopher, I hope someone told her that?" Pleading, almost begging. *Why did he have to come back?*

"Yeah, Hester did. That's why they did the family meetings. To set ground rules, so no one takes advantage of your abilities."

"Goddess, what's that mean...?" Dustin hated when his family made decisions on his behalf, without him present.

What was called the Ney family was an extended assortment of loosely related individuals and small clusters. Dustin's father Nate, had two brothers. Marlow who Dustin picked up pies from, was one. Dustin being single child escaped some of the family rivalry, but none of the attention. Single children families were uncommon on both sides. Marta's sister Ammogene, birthed several children by several people. Those collections were Dustin's cousins. Dustin after meeting Arman and the guys the morning after he and Al departed, gave Arman a refresher course in whom to expect at the house. It went so far over Arman's head that he left him to figure it out on his own.

Hester and Lucinda, Marta's moms each had one sister, who had messes of kids. Tomas and Jahnna, Nate's parents had more than a few siblings on both sides that resulted in even more family. Add the adopted children, friends and strays like Arman now was, Dustin's family could fill a medium-sized town.

So, because addressing issues in a fair manner was always a Ney tradition, an attempt at giving everyone a voice; family meetings tended to be lengthy with many folks in the house and conferencing on phones, tablets and by other means. Means they kept to themselves.

This conference was essentially a family reunion masquerading as a religious exploration of faith, for the purposes of writing the expenses off on the Ney family taxes. It amazed Dustin to no end that with all the scheming and hard work at subterfuge, his family wasn't wealthy. They shared the burdens and expenses collectively so everyone could have a standard of living that was acceptable but not extravagant. Those schemes and plots were up to the individual, and that was treated more like a game.

"It was decided that if you are now gifted, no one should expect special treatment, and if you volunteer your time, to run errands or what not... That's entirely up to you." Arman had a certain knowing look in his gaze. He'd seen what's behind the curtain now, and it was scary.

"Where's the list posted?"

"The wall in the main room in the apartment. You can't miss it."

"Fun." Dustin made bug eyes. Guilt to run stupid errands for his relatives. He should have stayed human.